Her Cold Heart

Cyborg Redemption

By Michelle Howard

Published by MH Publications

Also by Michelle Howard

A Novel of the Dracol

Rylin's Fire

Relentless Fire

Frost Fire

Secret Fire

Assassins Guild

The Unexpected Bonding Vow

Claiming His Unexpected Baby

His Unexpected Mate

A World Beyond

Torkel's Chosen

Torkels Auserwählte

Arak's Love

Arak's Liebe

Lindsey's Rescue

Kyele's Passion

Rydak's Fall
Jaron's Promise
V'hor's Nestmate
Stolen Moments
Bane's Heart
Nikol's Surrender

Cyborg Redemption
His Cold Kiss
Her Cold Heart

Le Cœur dans les étoiles
Union à tout prix
Amour à toute épreuve

Liebe in den Sternen
Animalische Begierde
Einzigartige Liebe

Love in the Stars
Mating Urge
Love Like No Other

Magical Lovers

Djinn Lover

Wicked Lover

Wild Lover

The Vassi Contact

As Darkness Spreads

As Dawn Rises

Un roman de L'univers Dracol

La Flamme de Rylin

La Flamme verte

La Flamme de glace

Un Roman di Dracol

il fuoco di Rylin

Fuoco Implacabile

Fuoco di Ghiaccio

Warlord Series

Honor Bound

The Overlord's Heir

A King's Revenge
Rise of the Shadow Warriors
A Warlord's Heart
Unexpected Bride
Unleashing A Warrior

Wired

Wired for Love

Standalone

No Reason To Run
Project Genesis

Watch for more at www.michellehowardwrites.com.

Cyborg Redemption

Michelle Howard- His Cold Kiss
Michelle Howard- Her Cold Heart
A.M. Griffin- Saving The Cyborg
Regine Abel- True As Steel
Lolita Lopez- Hijacked

Chapter 1

Cheers rose in the crowd and the screaming reached ear splitting decibels as the two men in the gladiator ring fought. Or rather, had fought. The match was as good as over.

Sora shook her head as the winner held up his opponent's limp body above his head, spun in a circle and heaved it. The body flew across the arena coming to a stop when it slammed into the ground with a dust rising, floor shaking thump.

Another cheer went up. This one louder than the others as the challenger remained unmoving. A clear indication this was the end of the match. Credits would be paid out to those who'd bet on the reigning champion. Farid Ogoni.

Farid didn't spare a glance at the audience who'd paid to see him fight on the *Gladyx*. The cruiser style ship traveled from location to location, never staying in one place for fear authorities would catch up to them.

Not because gladiator fights were illegal. Those matches were all the rage. No, the reason the *Gladyx* had to stay in motion was because the owners drafted contestants unwillingly.

Out of the thirty registered fighters, allegedly only four were here of their own free will. Farid was purported to be one of them.

As if finally noticing the screams, his gaze scanned the crowd. A harsh grimace etched his ruthless features in severe lines. Sora's heart sped up as she took in his massive form. The single weathered harness strung across his pectoral muscles looped over his shoulder and emphasized his intimidating form.

Sora wasn't intimidated but she certainly appreciated a fine form when she saw it. Two long black braids hung over his shoulders. As a Gurzal, his mottled brown and olive green skin would normally act as camouflage in the jungles on his home world. Here, it stood out in a sea of jewel toned races.

Each step he made out of the arena thudded, his bare feet not hesitating on the trek across the rough, blood-stained ground toward the entryway he'd come in through.

The knee length pants he wore were held up by a wide brown belt with the skull of some creature on the front. His heavily muscled thighs and calves drew her gaze down and she controlled a shiver. He could crush a being with his lower limbs alone and she was willing to bet he'd done that at least once in his time here. Maybe more.

A quick glance assured that the crowd was as enraptured with his silent and unemotional exit as Sora. When he reached the arched opening, he tipped his thick neck back. The roar he released sent the crowd into a renewed frenzy. She swore tremors shook the rafters though her internal sensors said they didn't.

"Magnificent, is he not?"

Sora turned slightly, keeping Farid in her field of vision as she eyed the being who'd approached on her left. The male wore a black coat tossed over one shoulder, revealing a one piece black jumper beneath. There were emblems on the left side of his chest but from this angle she couldn't make them out. His black boots were polished to a high sheen.

To answer his question, she gave a succinct nod and faced the arena again. The disguise as a wealthy buyer was masterful and if she hadn't been aware of his true identity, Kelix would have fooled her.

They'd come here in search of their missing pod members. Or rather from Kelix's pod. They'd received information that the last two cyborgs from his grouping had been forced into the gladiator fights. So far, neither of them had crossed paths with Kaito or Xion. She hoped the intel they'd received hadn't been wrong.

Their plan was to confirm if their fellow cyborgs were here, rescue them and leave. She and Kelix were running out of time if they were to escape undetected. The next stop for the *Gladyx* was the Hanass colony in eight days and Hanass had a strong relationship with her home planet, Kirs.

At her lengthy silence, Kelix sighed as if disappointed. "Looks like that was the last fight."

"Hmm," she hummed her noncommittal response under her breath, keeping up the charade of not knowing him.

"There's an electro-panel sparking in one of the soaking rooms," Kelix continued in a deep voice.

That was the coded phrase. She turned casually, one eye on Farid's disappearing form. Head down, chest heaving from his exertions, something about his posture tugged at her heartstrings and she couldn't figure out why. As a cyborg, a lot of her emotions had been suppressed to make her a better soldier but since the escape, they were slowly reawakening.

"I can look at it now," she murmured. "Can you show me where?"

Kelix, going by the name of Durwin Cantos, nodded slightly toward a hall behind them. "This way."

With one last look at Farid, her target, she walked away. There would be time tonight to approach him. His routine hadn't changed in the two weeks she'd been onboard. It would be easy to find him later in the private soak rooms easing his muscles.

Using her keycode, Sora entered the designated room and glanced around to make sure no one was inside. It was empty. She tipped her head to Kelix and he strode in, locking the door carefully behind him. "What did you find out?"

"Farid Ogoni and Tok Su have been here the longest. Tok is in the infirmary with cranial injuries after his fight tonight and not likely to survive. Farid's the one to speak to," she told him.

From public records, it was known that Farid joined the *Gladyx* cruiser in the early days and had been fighting for them for almost ten years. Offers from other fight rings to buy him were continually rejected. His contract was owned solely by the conglomerate and while they teased about lending him to other fights, he'd never left the ship.

Kelix grunted and folded his arms over his chest as he leaned against the wall and listened. Sora and Kelix had both gone undercover on the *Gladyx*. Sora as a repair mechanic in the maintenance department and Kelix as an eager buyer with a lot of credits looking to sponsor a fighter.

"When and how will you seek him out?" Kelix asked.

"Tonight. After a match like this one, he always comes to the soak rooms and stays for several hours."

Kelix's lips firmed. "I don't like you being alone with him. His reputation is well earned."

One thing Sora had discovered during their time undercover was that Kelix had a protective streak a kilometer wide. "I'm a cyborg and stronger than I look. Besides, any damage he could do would be healed by my nanobots."

Kelix pushed off the wall with a heavy sigh and dropped his arms. "That doesn't mean you can't be severely injured or even killed. We both know that."

For a moment, Sora's thoughts darkened. Kelix was right. They knew that better than many. Thalen, a member from her own pod, had placed himself in a repair sleep mode back at their temporary base on Solus. He'd sustained a level of damage his nanobots couldn't keep up with.

"I know, but outside of the ring and fights, Farid hasn't shown any sign of being more aggressive than anyone else on the *Gladyx*. In fact, his reputation outside of the arena is that of a loner who minds his business."

Kelix grunted and met her gaze, not agreeing or disagreeing with her statement. His dark eyes burned with the same ferocity probably reflected in hers. "Keep me posted on whatever you find out and let me know when you're safely in your room."

"Right."

"I'll leave first," Kelix said, then eased the door open. He looked left then right before going through without a backward glance at Sora.

As soon as the door closed, she went to a specific section on the wall and crouched. Placing her palm on the electro-panel that controlled the lighting and temperature for this room, she pushed a bit of energy forward.

Push was the only word she'd ever managed that came close to describing what she did with the surfeit of energy constantly bubbling beneath the surface of her skin.

From what she could tell, no other cyborg had a similar ability. Sora didn't publicize it often and until the emperor of Kirs had gone on his mad rampage, no one else aside from her pod had known.

Now Kelix and the four others she'd banded with knew because Sora had used her skill to escape the transport taking them all to a prison colony unjustly.

Sparks flared from the panel, shorting out the electronics on the other side. Standing quickly, she wiped her hands on the pants of her uniform jumper and hurried to the door. The issue would register on the system and the head of her department would see it.

Later, he'd send her out to do the repair thus giving her the necessary reason to be here when she propositioned Farid.

***

Closing his eyes, Farid leaned his head back to rest on the rim of the soaking tub and groaned. From head to toe, his entire body ached. The match with the Umden had drained him more than he expected. As to his opponents' death, not even a gleam of remorse poked at his conscience. Guilt had been left far behind after Farid's second year onboard the *Gladyx* as an indentured fighter on behalf of the conglomerate.

According to Garod, a member of the three-person entity, who held his fighter contract, Farid had taken longer than others to succumb to the inevitable. He'd learned though.

Learned to adapt and adjust to the brutal life he'd been forced into and survival stayed at the forefront of his mind.

Nothing was going to stop Farid from winning his last fights. Just two more. Then he'd be free of his ten year commitment. Once done, Farid could walk away and breathe easy. His fingers clenched on the rim of the tub. Freedom was finally in reach along with the attainment of his secret goal.

The door opened and closed behind him. Farid's senses went on alert but he didn't betray his awareness by so much as a twitch. While rare, occasionally buyers and passengers tried to sneak into fighter only spaces.

Most wanted the privilege of meeting someone they equated with fame, some wanted sex and others hoped to bribe him to throw a match.

Staying loose and limber, his ears strained as light steps crossed the tiled space. There were several soaking tubs that others could use after matches but because Farid's fights were considered major highlights they occurred late. It could have been another competitor but they would have already come through and left by now.

When his name wasn't called and steps didn't come near him, he inhaled and tentatively relaxed. A hinge squeaked. Shuffling noises followed then a muttered curse in the Standard language generally spoken.

The layout of the room filtered through his mind. A security panel and electronic board were located where the sounds came from. Along with the scent of musk and a metallic tang, he surmised that one of the maintenance techs had entered.

Easing his lids open a crack, he tipped his head to the side, barely disturbing the heated water. Shapely firm buttocks encased in dull green uniform pants greeted him. Bent over the panel as the female was, he had a good view, so Farid stared at the individual a moment longer.

"Sorry," she called out in a lyrical voice.

He stirred and shifted. He hadn't expected her to speak. Workers on the traveling cruiser didn't tend to speak to the fighters, too intimidated and afraid of being attacked.

Farid withheld a snort. Fights broke out all the time without a word being spoken. Sometimes a wrong look would do.

The only thing keeping fighters in check was the remote controlled explosive device implanted in each of their wrists. Death by spontaneous combustion wasn't high on anyone's way to die.

"I'll only be a few more minutes," she continued, shifting her ass about as she squatted and pulled several tools from the large bag he hadn't initially noticed beside her booted feet.

Tiny feet. Farid's hand could probably span the entire length of one.

"You're one of the quiet ones, huh?" she chatted, undeterred by his lack of response.

Her hands moved swiftly, exchanging a part for another and inserted a chip in the slot on the side. She was obviously experienced at her job and seemed to complete the actions by rote.

At any other time, Farid would have turned away by now, safe in the assumption she was no danger to him. She carried the right scent—a mix of machinery and oils with a touch of muted chemicals.

Even what she wore fit, the right amount of wear on the one-piece uniform and minor stains to attest to her workday. But one thing gave away her ruse. Those shoes containing her tiny feet, which had caught his attention, were unmarked. No scuffs or worn tread to reflect the time she spent running from one end of the ship to the other, depending on where she was assigned.

Granted, they could be new, her old pair worn out, but she'd gone through so much trouble to look well established in her role that it stood out. And when things stood out, Farid paid attention. He couldn't afford to slip up. His wasn't the only life at stake.

"Who are you?" he asked, rising slowly from the soaker and facing her.

Water slewed down his body, the heat in the room pumping at a rate to guarantee he didn't feel the slightest chill.

The maintenance woman stiffened and glanced over her shoulder at him. Smoke gray eyes, sharp cheek bones and full pouty lips painted deep red, faced him. He catalogued her looks even as he tensed to defend himself if necessary.

Something on his face must have warned her of the danger she was in. She turned and stood, a torquing wrench held loosely in her right hand. Farid's lips curled up at the defensive gesture. In response, her eyes narrowed.

"Sora. I work in maintenance," she answered his question at last.

"Why are you in here this late?"

She shrugged and pointed over her shoulder with her free hand. "There was a flag in the system. Whenever an alert like that goes off, we have to check it out. This one had a blown conductor for the heat coils under the soaker tubs."

Farid didn't care about a single thing she'd just said. It was her body language that caught his attention. She held her posture in a loose stance but her watchful gray eyes never wavered from his and her hold on the tool remained at the ready.

She was no ordinary repair person. Farid had noted all of them and none worked as quickly or efficiently as she had and none came out this late for a minor tech issue.

More than that, not one individual on this ship would be bold enough to hold a potential weapon at the ready to fight back against the top champion in the *Gladyx* ring. So, for that and the new boots, she warranted a closer look.

He climbed from the water, unconcerned with his nudity and reached for a towel to knot casually around his waist. Every deliberate step he took, closed the distance between them. The tech, or Sora as she'd said but could be a lie, didn't blanch. Farid stopped in front of her with mere inches to spare. "Who are you?"

She jerked. Then blew out a breath. "I already told you but for some reason you've decided I'm lying and are using your stature and reputation to intimidate me."

While her tone wasn't scolding, he took it as such. For one brief second, a flare of shame coursed through him. There had been a time when he hadn't treated women like that. He immediately shut down the feeling.

There was no room for manners if there was a threat to his end goal. He reached out, expecting her to pull away or swing the torquing wrench in his direction. She didn't move or flinch.

Nerves of steel. A sizzle of attraction slid down Farid's spine and he ruthlessly quelled it. He cupped her jaw in his rough palm and leaned in close. "Are you intimidated?"

A split second later, Farid froze.

"Do I look intimidated?" she asked with a deliberate smile and a flutter of those long lashes.

Farid glanced down. Her hand had a tight grip on his cock beneath the towel. She wasn't applying pressure but her clasp warned that could change at a moment's notice.

"I need to end my shift. Sorry to have disturbed you." Her sultry voice lured with every word she spoke and he was certain she knew it. Releasing him, she backed away and gathered her tool box.

When she walked out the door, she was whistling. Farid had to force himself not to chase after her to see if he could tease out another side of her. Change the efficient tech into a wanton who would beg for his touch. It was what he would have done before.

But those days were gone. He sighed, shoulders drooping in fatigue. Farid only spent time with women if they knew the deal and wouldn't be around to try and change his mind. He didn't think the tech fit those parameters. While workers tended to come and go onboard, the maintenance techs lasted the longest.

Alone in the steamy room, Farid shook his head and went to retrieve his clothes. For the first time in a long time, he was intrigued. Too bad he didn't have time for distractions.

Chapter 2

"We haven't seen any sign of Kaito and Xion but that might change. Today is the day new fighters are supposed to be introduced to the audience," Sora reported on her comm.

She glanced at Kelix. They'd managed to meet in the tiny suite she'd been assigned since she wasn't scheduled to work today. His room was on a different level with other high-end guests and would draw too much attention.

On the comm, Cyllus sighed. "I'd hoped we'd know something by now. You and Kelix have already been gone for over two weeks."

Cyllus and Kelix belonged to the same cyborg pod. This was hard on both of them. They wanted Kaito and Xion to be here so they could save their missing brethren but they also didn't want them to be here on the *Gladyx* because of the abuse alleged.

Some of the matches were to the death and the fighters to her knowledge didn't receive compensation. Knowing that, why would any sensible being agree to fight on the traveling cruiser? There was no logic to it which meant something was off.

Beside her, Kelix paced in her room and told Cyllus, "I tried to access them via our NNP but couldn't get through. If they were in range, I should be able to talk to them."

Their implanted neural net processor allowed them to communicate directly cyborg to cyborg with members in their pod. The connection should have worked.

"At least we know they aren't dead," Cyllus said.

It was the only bright side they had to cling to right now. Sora hadn't been able to connect to the two still missing from her pod. She'd found one, Thalen, back on Solus. After taking serious damage from escaping the exploding transports they'd been on, he remained unresponsive while his body recovered.

Who knew how long it would take him to wake from the repair mode he'd put himself in so his nanobots could work faster?

"Let me know as soon as you find out. Tagan and I can be there quickly," Cyllus was saying as Sora focused.

Tagan was another cyborg who'd escaped with them. Stubborn and belligerent, he'd surprisingly ended up being the one who agreed to watch Thalen for her. It eased Sora's mind to know the harsh cyborg guarded her friend. Thalen was as close as a brother to her and they'd grown up together.

"If we don't discover Kaito and Xion with the fighters today, we'll give it another week and leave. We can't afford to be caught on Hanass. Sora and I have been over every inch of this ship except the lower deck where select fighters are housed. Authorized access is restricted to the conglomerate members running the *Gladyx* and a few guards and crew. I haven't been able to bribe my way in."

Kelix had tried but gotten nowhere. Sora had tried too, pretending maintenance repairs but was denied. That section had its own maintenance crew.

If only they could get eyes in there to search for Kaito and Xion. Or at least talk to the other fighters to ask if they'd seen them or knew something.

Which brought to mind Farid. The soaking room incident was the closest Sora had managed to get to any of the fighters and he'd been suspicious and on guard from the moment she entered.

"Sora?"

Sora blinked when Kelix said her name. She'd followed the conversation even as her mind had wandered. "Yes?"

"Did you have any luck with Farid the other night?"

"No. He was suspicious of my presence but I hope to try again. There has to be a way to convince someone to talk to us." Sora had hinted heavily with her fellow repair techs but most of them had no idea what was going on. They only wanted to get paid and keep their heads down. Sora couldn't blame them.

"Any word about Reo?" she asked.

The other cyborg who'd been with them when they made their escape had vanished, leaving a simple message behind. They hoped to find him as well since Reo's pod members were all dead. To her knowledge, he didn't have anyone else to look out for him.

"No." Cyllus grunted. "We haven't heard anything but I've got feelers out and Tagan's working himself to exhaustion reviewing the passenger lists for every ship that left that morning."

"Cyllus, I have to go. I'm supposed to join a group of buyers for drinks. I'll try my luck there," Kelix said.

"Good luck to both of you." Cyllus ended the comm.

Sora met Kelix's midnight eyes. He smoothed his dark hair back from a remarkably handsome face and slid his hands deep into his pants pockets. Facial prosthetics covered his cheekbones, giving them a fuller shape.

They both wore the cosmetic enhancement to hide the permanent brand forced on them by the emperor of their home world. If anyone saw the scarred CR lettering, they'd instantly know Sora and Kelix were runaway cyborg rebels.

She could see the pain and frustration Kelix couldn't quite hide. This was wearing on him. It was evident Kelix had expected to arrive and rescue his brethren right away. The longer it took, the more worried he became about their fate.

"You good?" she asked when he didn't immediately say anything.

The bland mask he used in his persona as wealthy buyer without a care slipped firmly back in place. His transition from worried cyborg to arrogant buyer was seamless. Even the smirk he wore spoke of conceit if she didn't know any better. "Sure. I'll sneak out now before the halls get crowded and the excitement about the introductions brings out the lurkers."

"I hope they're here, Kelix."

Persona faltering for a split second, his lips flattened then he nodded. "Thanks."

He eased open the door and slid out. Sora waited a sufficient amount of time, then left and locked up behind her, though she knew it didn't matter. Her room had been searched her first day onboard and every other day since more or less. Someone had access to her private space so she did her best not to leave anything incriminating around.

Going down the hall, Sora kept her gaze straight ahead, taking note of the newer patrons who'd joined the ship since their last stop two days ago. All were excited to catch the first glimpse of the additional fighters who would be in the upcoming matches.

New fighters were a common occurrence considering many died during the highly watched death battles. Some were injured severely in the regular bouts and unable to fight despite the top notch medical care they received.

The one time she'd faked an ailment to get inside the medical facilities, Sora had used her internal scanner on the equipment and whistled. She couldn't speak to the mental and emotional state but the conglomerate appeared to want those who fought in the best *physical* condition possible.

"Sora, I was on my way to your room. You're alert isn't on," Dottie said.

Dottira, *please call me Dottie*, worked in maintenance with Sora. The other female smiled often and seemed to keep an upbeat attitude no matter how often Sora made it clear she wasn't looking to make friends.

"I'm off today," Sora told her, drawing to a stop in the hall.

"Ah, well that explains it. There's an urgent repair request in and Simin insists that you be the one to respond."

Simin was their supervisor and talked to the team as if they were trash beneath his booted feet. Sora would love five minutes alone with him to show him a few things.

Instead, she feigned a smile for Dottie who wasn't responsible. She just got stuck delivering the message. "I can't, Dottie. I'm going to grab something to eat then head to the arena on the lower level for a good seat to watch the introductions."

While there, Sora would do her best to search the holding pens as they were called. *If* she could get one of the guards to let her through. The introduction event only happened once and for a short period of time. She didn't want to miss Kaito and Xion if they were here.

Fear flashed across Dottie's pale face. "Oh, you have to, Sora. It's one of the fighter's rooms. Simin made it clear it has to be fixed correctly and we've all learned that you're unmatched on electrical issues."

A fighter's room? Sora hummed under her breath. This could be the break they needed. "Which fighter?"

"Farid Ogoni." Dottie shivered saying the name and rubbed her arms briskly. "He scares me."

This was too good to be true. Sora blew out a breath as if put out. "Fine. I'll do it but Simin has to make sure I get paid for the time on the clock. As for the rest of my day, I'll be out of reach. He needs to understand that."

Sora didn't want it to look like she gave in too easy. Simin was sure to ask Dottie for a detailed report on Sora's response, expression and any other details he thought might reveal something he could use to coerce Sora in the future.

She'd seen him do the other techs like that. Find something they cared about, some minor mistake they made, then hold it over their heads to force them to do what he wanted. Often without pay.

"Thank you, Sora! It sounds like a simple call too. He's due in the arena later and rumor is, he's pretty heated about the delay."

Chapter 3

The pounding at Farid's door was a relief. His power was out and he was running late. He stormed across his room and swung the door open. Surprise flashed through him when he saw the pretty tech from the soaking room.

"Hi, I'm responding to the service alert regarding your lights," she said when he didn't move out of the way.

Farid stepped to the side, holding the door open with his arm stretched across the top. She entered with no hesitation despite the pitch-black room. He could barely see yet she unerringly headed through his living room area and into the small kitchen he rarely used.

Bemused, Farid followed, watching his step to keep from tripping. He couldn't afford to fall and risk an injury before his next fight.

"You in a hurry?" the tech said.

What was her name? She'd told him but he couldn't remember. Last night had been a bad one. Between the death match, the strained muscles and his growing concern about his next two fights, he hadn't been in a good place.

"I have to be at the show shortly."

"Show?" she peered at him over her shoulder and chuckled. "Never heard it called that before."

Her laughter sent shivers down his spine. "Yes. Lots of unnecessary fanfare."

Today would be a bunch of grimacing on his part and playing to the crowd. The members of the conglomerate knew not to expect too much from Farid during these introduction sessions. Their agreement was straightforward and to the point. He'd give them ten years of his life without protest or attempts to escape and at the end of that time frame, they gave him what he wanted and his freedom.

"Well. I might be a few minutes but you shouldn't be too late," she muttered, going to her knees to remove the grate at the bottom of his kitchen wall.

Fuck, it was dark in here.

"Should you use a tube light?" he asked, wondering how she expected to fix anything if she couldn't see.

She grunted a response then reached behind her and pulled out a silver tube from her back pocket. A bright stream of white flicked on and she aimed it into the recesses of the wall.

Farid crossed his arms over his chest and leaned a shoulder against the column separating the kitchen from his living room. Until he'd mentioned it, she didn't seem to need the light. She also didn't have her bag with her this time. Suspicion returned and he tensed. "What did you say your name was again?"

Her hesitation lasted so long Farid dropped his arms to his sides in preparation. If members of the conglomerate had sent Sora as a spy or to weaken him in some way before his next fight, he would decimate her despite his attraction.

Nothing could interfere with his plan. If he lost either of these last two fights, the agreement he had was null and void and he'd be stuck on the *Gladyx* fighting for the rest of his life. Worse than that, he'd lose the most important thing to him, the only reason he pushed himself harder and harder to win.

"Sora. My name is Sora."

Sora. He mouthed the name silently. No last name, he noted. Then again she didn't owe him that.

"What were you doing when the lights blew?"

She remained in a crouched position as she asked the question. Farid came closer to hear her better. "Nothing. I dressed and was about to leave to head to the arena when it suddenly went dark."

She mumbled something he couldn't hear and leaned forward, half her body inside the opening into the wall. The position arched her back and popped her curvy ass upward.

Farid's vision wasn't great in the dark and he regretted that fact more than ever right now. Impatient to have the matter resolved or saved until later, he parted his lips to tell her to come back another time when she scooted backward. At the same time, the lights above flickered on and the hum of the cooling system reactivated.

"All done," she said, standing up and brushing at her thighs.

Her dark hair was ruffled and there was a streak of dirt on her left cheek. Farid controlled the need to wipe it clean and test the softness of her skin. The pale gold tone shimmered beneath the lighting. Thick lashes lined wide gray eyes and her bottom lip formed an attractive pout.

She wasn't in her customary uniform. If he thought the bland green jumper highlighted her sleek form, it was nothing compared to the white half shirt she wore, baring her middle and the low slung black pants that hung on her hips and hugged her thighs. Stirrings of desire poked at his senses.

"It was a loose wire. Do you need me to look at anything else?" she prodded.

Farid realized he'd been staring. "No. Wait. In my bedroom, the vid unit flickers on and off. I've had techs in here a few times and it will work for a day or two then go back to flickering."

The broken vid unit was more an annoyance than anything. Farid didn't watch many programs or news clips but the delay would allow him to spend more time with...Sora. Something about her didn't align with the image she projected and Farid didn't like when things or people didn't align.

***

Farid's unwavering stare caused goosebumps to break out over Sora's arms. She swallowed and used her processors to keep her heart rate steady and her breathing even. His impact on her senses was unexpected and stronger than when they crossed paths in the soaking room.

As one of the top contenders in the arena and with the largest fan following, she'd been watching him since her arrival on the ship. After studying dozens of other fighters to question, she'd settled on Farid and hoped he could be the one to help her. She hadn't counted on the unexpected attraction or his unnerving suspicion.

Standing before her in a plain rough spun white shirt and dark loose fitting pants, his presence wasn't as dominating as it was in the arena. Not that he wasn't physically as imposing. He definitely was. Nothing could minimize his hulking frame and all that smooth brown and green skin.

But the lack of aggression, the relaxed stance and his chest being covered by an actual shirt offered a different perspective.

If only she could break through the distant manner he projected. Looking for an excuse to delay leaving, she asked, "It was a loose wire. Do you need me to look at anything else?"

"No. Wait. In my bedroom, the vid unit flickers on and off. I've had techs in here a few times and it will work for a day or two then go back to flickering."

Sora expected an immediate denial. In fact, she' already turned to make her way to the door when his words filtered in. "Oh. Well, if other techs looked, I'm not sure what I could do but I'll check if you want."

His lips curled on one side, flashing potent dimples that took his looks up and beyond the hot scale as he growled out, "You're here, might as well."

A ringing endorsement. Holding in the desire to roll her eyes, Sora inclined her head. "If you'll show me the way. I don't have my tools but maybe it's a simple fix like this."

Farid moved with surprising grace for one of his size. She shouldn't be surprised. In the ring, he displayed an ease and level of raw power, battling his opponents with ruthless skill and style.

She entered his bedroom and the scent of him immediately assaulted her nasal passages. Heavy, dark with a rich hint of spices her processors couldn't identify.

"Over here," he said, standing next to a wall mounted screen with a blank blue display.

Shaking off the distraction brought on by being surrounded by the essence of Farid, Sora crossed to his side and eyed the vid unit. "You said it flickers?"

"The image. Whenever it's on." He demonstrated by using a remote and turning it on.

News blurbs came to life in a loud staccato blast of audio. Farid's thumbs mashed at the remote until the sound lowered. "Sorry."

Two red slashes appeared on his greenish brown cheeks. His awkwardness was endearing. Sora smiled. "Let me have a look."

She went to the vid unit and pulled it away from the wall using the extendable arm. As soon as she moved it, Sora realized the problem. Now how to handle it. She could mention it to Farid to gain his trust, ignore it—the smart option, or destroy it and pretend it was an accident if questioned.

"Is it something you can fix?"

Sora cleared her throat and eased the screen back to the wall. "I think I can handle it but I'll need a part. I can come back tomorrow unless it's urgent."

He looked from her to the vid unit then back again. Questions rose in his eyes but all he said was, "Tomorrow works."

"Great." Sora forced a smile to her face and walked away. As she neared the door of his bedroom, she tripped.

Farid caught her mid-fall. His arms wrapped around her waist and he pulled her up. "Are you alright?"

"There's a camera behind your vid unit," Sora murmured.

Chapter 4

Though his eyes flared at the discovery, Farid proved he wasn't only a strong body and that there was a brain attached. With a light squeeze to her forearms confirming he'd heard, he helped her up and stepped away. "I'll walk you out."

Side by side, they made their way into the living area, pass the kitchen nook and out the door, Farid locking it behind him. In the hall, he faced her and asked, "How do you know?"

Insulted, Sora scrunched her nose. "I can do this job with my eyes closed. Recognizing recording devices is a child's skill."

Farid braced his hands on his hips and eyed her from head to toe, taking in the white crop top she wore and the lightweight pants she favored for the ease of movement they gave her. "Who are you and why did you tell me?"

Sora masked her surprise at his questions. She'd hoped informing him would create a bond she could use to endear him to her. Instead, it seemed to have increased his suspicions. Holding up her hands in the universal sign of surrender, she gave him the truth. "I told you because I assumed you weren't aware. That micro-bug is more than likely the reason you can't get a stable image on the holo-vids you watch."

He huffed out an annoyed breath then scanned the hall around them. There were a few stragglers making their way about. No one paid any attention to them. He turned back to her. "I have to get ready for check-in along with the other fighters. When I'm done, we're going to talk."

He said the last in an ominous tone before turning and striding away. Sora cursed under her breath and followed at a slower pace. They were going to the same location but she didn't want to incur his wrath by staying on his heels. Her goal was to work *with* him not against him.

Entering the arena reminded Sora of how huge the fighting venue was. Already dozens of travelers occupied rows and rows of seats. Head up, she walked with confidence to the arched entryway that led to the holding pens below where the fighters prepped in advance.

Today there wouldn't be any prep but it was the perfect opportunity to investigate the new arrivals. At the entry, a different guard stood watch, eyeing her approach. "Sorry, authorized personnel only."

Sora tossed her hair back and smiled shyly. "I only wanted to get a look at the new fighters."

Haersutes were covered in hair all over their body and his long strands wavered about his body as he looked around. Three beady black eyes returned to her. "You work in repair and maintenance, right?"

Wondering how he knew, Sora nodded and widened her smile. "Yes. That's me."

He glanced around again and chewed his bottom lip. "Is something broken down here? Nobody said anything."

He was clearly new and didn't know there was a separate maintenance team assigned specifically to this section. Not wanting to lie outright and risk getting him in trouble, Sora shrugged. "Since I was already here to see the intros, I figured I'd take a look around to make sure everything was alright."

A relieved smile crossed his hairy face. "Well. Alright. I'm new here, but I guess that would be okay."

Victory was a heady feeling. Previous guards had been adamant and didn't let anyone in.

Sora waved and strolled through as if she had the right to be here though she wasn't in her uniform. If anyone asked, she'd use the same story she told the guard. Her off day and checking on things.

The underground of the arena reminded her of a prison colony building. Eight by eight spaces allotted to each contender just like prison cells. The only difference was that there were no doors or bars here. At least not in the first open cells she passed but they were occupied by growling, snarling men in various states of dress. Some paced angrily back and forth, some sat on the floor quietly waiting.

Several alien races were present. A few had a vague resemblance to humanoids even the Cepphi with his multiple tentacles and the blue-skinned Zudan with his six arms waving around. None of them seemed eager to escape or as if they were being held against their will.

Guards casually strolled down the center aisle, no weapons in sight to stop a fighter if they did decide to bolt. A few even nodded to her in acknowledgment when they recognized her.

Sora had made it a point to be visible and constantly volunteered for repairs throughout the ship. It gave her a chance to scout but also to familiarize herself with those onboard. She wasn't quite friendly because that invited personal questions but she made it appear as if she was a hard worker looking to please.

At the midway point of the aisle, the cells or rooms, she guessed she'd call them, changed. The next ones were enclosed cages. She couldn't tell what the reasoning was for the difference unless it was the occupants.

Were they more dangerous? The new fighters?

Her pulse kicked up. Maybe she was finally getting somewhere.

Keeping an eye out for any nearby guard, Sora approached the first barred cell on her left. The gray skinned male inside leaned against the wall, head cocked in her direction. A single eye in the middle of his forehead watched her every step. He wore a loincloth and boots.

"Hello," Sora said and stopped in front of his cage.

Ignoring etiquette, he snapped, "What are you doing down here?"

Dropping her nice routine, Sora propped her hands on her hips and lowered her voice. She didn't need to draw any attention to them. "I'm having a look around. I don't remember seeing you before."

He grunted and propped a foot on the wall behind him then folded his arms over his chest. "And?"

Damn it. "And I wanted to know if you're one of the new fighters being introduced today."

His single eye blinked. "Why?"

Lean and bald, she would have recalled if she'd seen him fight before. He *was* new. She and Kelix had attended every match they could while here. "Just curious."

He snorted and turned to look straight ahead at the empty wall on the opposite end of his cage. "Go be curious elsewhere."

Sora cautioned herself not to push. "Fine."

She moved to the next cage. Inside a huge man sat on the ground, staring. Silent tears rolled down the sharp angles of his cheeks. His blue eyes tipped up at the corners and widened when he saw Sora.

Another new fighter. She was sure. "Hello."

"Hello." His voice was whisper soft and light like bells.

She couldn't identify what he was. His tanned skin and dark hair could have belonged to any number of beings. Horns curled back from a prominent forehead but the standout feature was his size. If he stood, his head would touch the top of the bars. He had to be twice Farid Ogoni's size.

"Are you new?"

"I don't belong here," he murmured gently.

Such a sweet voice for a man with his rugged muscle bound physique.

"What's your name?" Sora asked, glancing around with a wary eye.

"Zozo."

No time to waste. Sora got straight to the point. "That's nice. Do you want to leave, Zozo?"

He sniffed and wiped at a tear. Bracing one large fist on the ground he leaned his weight forward and excitement flickered in his formerly dull gaze. "I can leave?"

"I think if you want, you can. Unless there's a reason you have to fight."

Tell me something. Anything.

Zozo leaned back and his shoulders slumped. "I can't leave."

"Why?"

He didn't answer.

"Zozo?"

Sora didn't get a response. He was back to staring off into the distance. Controlling a growl of frustration, Sora headed to the next cage.

"Hey! The shows about to start what are you doing down here?"

A guard with leathery brown skin and pointed ears on top of his head ambled in her direction. Sora pushed her lips up in a jovial grin though she wanted to pound his face for interrupting. "Sorry. Taking a quick look around."

His thick brows drew together. "You're with the maintenance crew. No one called in a repair and you're not in uniform."

Music started in the arena. It was time for her to go anyway. Sora stayed relaxed and waved. "I'm leaving now."

She didn't glance at Zozo or the cyclops being as she headed for the stadium seating area.

In the bright light of the arena, Sora took a deep breath and let it out. That had been risky and she was no closer to finding Kelix's two pod mates. If only she'd had the chance to see occupants in the rest of the cages.

And where had Farid and some of the other higher rated fighters been? Farid said he *had* to be here. Unless they were kept separate?

She spotted a section out in the front with two free seats remaining and made her way over. When she arrived, guests ignored her to comment on the current fighters.

"I like Tok Su but his injury has him sidelined from today's show," one man said, flipping through a digital holo-program suspended in the air.

Pretending nonchalance and an interest in the empty field, Sora tuned in to the conversation.

"Surprised he survived that major head injury. Had his skull cracked wide open. I'm more interested in the new fighters. We all know the current team. I'd like to see who's coming in and if any of them will be able to knock Farid Ogoni from the top of the food chain," another said.

The group of four nodded at this.

The first man lowered his hand, leaving the digital program up to be viewed. Sora scanned the names quickly and recognized most. There weren't any names listed for the incoming fighters. She hadn't expected to see any. The *Gladyx* preferred the surprise factor.

"Is anyone sitting here?" a familiar voice asked.

Sora met Kelix's gaze and shook her head. "No."

"Thanks." He sat and faced forward.

Later, Sora would tell him about her discovery of the listening device in Farid's room. Now wasn't the time but she had a ton of questions. Were the *Gladyx* owners concerned about his private time? Did they have a reason to worry? Any edge Sora could find would be beneficial.

Music blared from the speakers and the crowd screamed. People leaped to their feet and stomped. Names of favored fighters rang out and through it all, an electric current filled the air.

Sora stood to blend in and clapped enthusiastically though she was sickened by the production of it all. Introductions started with the current fighters. Deafening cheers came in waves. Each fighter sauntered or postured on their way to the center of the field below.

Until the last fighter was introduced.

"Farid Oooogoniiii!"

The sounds that followed raised the hair on Sora's head.

"Farid! Farid! Farid!"

She'd known he was popular. His matches were always touted as not to be missed especially if he took part in a death bout. With so many new passengers onboard from their previous stop, the appreciative shouts were louder than usual and blasted her sensitive auditory systems. Beside her, Kelix winced.

Walking behind Farid to the center of the arena were three men in sleek black one piece suits that molded to their lean forms. The men made up the conglomerate which controlled the *Gladyx*. It was the first time she'd noted them attending a match in person and she stored each of their faces to her databanks.

They were of the same race. Spikes ran up the sides of their necks, gold skin gleamed and their fluffy looking hair was cut close to their enlarged heads.

The one in the middle raised his black gloved hand for quiet. His crooked smile and narrowed gaze caused Sora a moment of unease. She glanced around to see if any others picked up on the weird vibe. Apparently, the audience's glee overruled any concern or worry.

Anger slashed at her chest. The rapid hunger and sheer greed to bet on brutal fights without thought to the participants enraged her. Kelix's shoulder brushed hers and she looked up. His dark eyes held a question and Sora shook her head. There was nothing to say. Kelix shared her disgust at this entire enterprise.

The idea that two men from his pod group could be here, men he considered brothers, left both of them ready to tear this place down.

"Thank you all for attending our annual new introduction day. I'm your host for the festivities, Garod. My partners, Urson, Parsons, and I are pleased to share our highest new arrival numbers ever with thirteen additional fighters."

More cheers and shouts along with stomping. Sora eyed the arena, wondering how any of them would react if they were taken from friends and family and forced to fight against their will.

Crew, buyers and owners laughed and pounded each other on the backs for being here. No guilt, just pleasure at the expense of another being. Heartless.

"Without further ado, I present Bindor. Bindor is our first Nagani contender from the forests of Njon. He's considered a prime male on his home world and we're excited to have him."

Garod's introduction implied Bindor had volunteered to be here. Not likely. The rumors that *Gladyx* fighters weren't always offered a choice didn't just pop up for no reason. She gritted her teeth in frustration. They needed Farid's help.

Buyers came from far and wide with credits to spend in hopes of finding an opponent who could break Farid's undefeated record of 543-0. All had failed. His reputation as ruthless in the arena hadn't been inflated. Sora had watched all of the matches he'd been in and he'd decimated the opposing fighters. Someone like him, surely knew more about the enterprise here.

"Any luck?" Kelix murmured at her side.

Keeping her gaze forward, Sora said, "I still haven't had the chance to talk in depth with him but I found a listening device in his bedroom."

She sensed the intensity of Kelix's stare at the news. "Listening device?"

"I'll fill you in later. He wants to talk." There'd been a threat implied when Farid said he'd see Sora.

Kelix grunted in acknowledgment. Farid had walked the perimeter of the arena by now and finally drew near them. He didn't wave as the others did, just glared into the audience. Until his gaze landed on Sora.

Heat flared between them. Attraction and sexual awareness bloomed deep in her belly. Sora swallowed but stood tall under his perusal. His regard caused her insides to quiver.

As much as he stared at her, Sora stared at him. Shirtless, he flexed his chest muscles and she inhaled sharply. Cyborgs had impressive physiques. Muscles and beautifully built bodies weren't new to Sora but Farid's cut form rippled with power.

Firm lines defined every inch of his upper body. His arms were thick from his broad shoulders down to his forearms.

Her reaction to the large fighter shouldn't be this strong. Kelix and Cyllus didn't believe in doing anything by half measure and the reports on each fighter contained as much information as they could gather. She'd had ample time to study Farid prior to arriving on the *Gladyx* ship.

But her libido wasn't listening. She needed to control this response to him, if only to avoid making a mistake. The risk still existed that Kelix and Sora could be caught but she hoped to avoid that.

If they happened to bring down the conglomerate along the way, all the better.

Farid's hazel eyes dropped to her bare midsection and stayed. Her nipples perked beneath the crop top she wore and she shifted her stance to ease the growing ache between her thighs. Her desire rose fiercely and she engaged her processors to shut down the sensations, dimming the arousal instantly.

Once those in the seats near her noticed how close he stood, they started chanting louder. "Farid! Farid!"

"At least you seem to have caught his interest. That can only work in your favor," Kelix murmured, seeing the attention given to her.

Farid's gaze slid to her left and stopped on Kelix. His eyes suddenly narrowed, the green overpowering the brown.

After another drawn moment between them, Farid completed his circle and ended back where he'd started in a line with the other fighters. At his approach, Garod wore a smug smile before speaking to the crowd again.

With her ocular implants, Sora couldn't miss the way Farid stiffened. His expression remained neutral but tension ran through his frame and locked his legs in their wide legged stance.

Discord. It gave her the first glimpse of an opening she could use.

Chapter 5

Farid didn't know why seeing the pretty maintenance tech seated next to the buyer, Durwin Cantos, bothered him so much. He'd put thoughts of desire and females to the back of his mind long ago thanks to Ashme. The former female fighter had taught him a harsh lesson ten years ago, one he would *never* forget.

Now the gray eyed tech drew his attention when he was close to freedom. He couldn't let himself be distracted no matter how much she appealed to a long-buried need.

Though his cock wasn't listening, going so far as to harden even now at the sight of her.

"We're going to bring out the new fighters next, Farid. Do your best to growl and pretend you want to attack them," Garod muttered in an aside while smiling at the audience.

The members of the conglomerate didn't often show up at the arena. This was a special occasion. New fighters were only introduced when the current stock ran low. Over a dozen men had perished in fights over the last month. The highest number in the shortest span of time since Farid had been here.

Garod and his friends had gotten greedy and upped the number of death matches. The thrill, the rush, whatever it was that drove them was hitting record highs. Farid curled his fingers at his side and gritted his teeth. Time was ticking and one day he'd be the one carried off the field.

He knew Garod hoped for that to happen preferably before Farid's last two fights. If he died before finishing his contract, the upset would bring in a flood of credits for the *Gladyx* and Garod wouldn't have to relinquish his prize.

The thought filled Farid with a mix of anger and terror. He had to survive. Surviving meant winning. And winning meant killing the fighters who stood around him.

"Now, everyone, please quiet down and welcome our newest additions." Garod grinned broadly, taking in the glory of the attention.

His partners were less obnoxious about the display but Urson and Parson were as guilty as Garod for running these forced fight games. If Farid could wrap his hands around the bastard's throat and end things now, he would.

"First we have a Doorian. The cyclops beings are notorious for being cold-blooded fighters without mercy. Not often do they leave their home world but fortune smiled on us and we have one with us today. Let's hear it for Bommba." Garod pointed toward the arched entry with a flourish.

All eyes followed. Farid clasped his hands behind his back and waited. He hadn't seen any of the new fighters yet. That wasn't unusual. Garod liked the surprise of the process and hoped this theatrical display would create excitement and fear to drive the betting up for the audience. Fighters too usually got caught up in the hype.

In the early years, it worked on Farid. He'd worried with each crop of new opponents, wondering if the one to beat him and destroy his whole world was there. Now, Farid knew better. Worry was akin to defeat.

With each fight, he grew stronger, smarter. His refusal to kill in the arena faded. Guilt for his actions dimmed.

It wasn't that Farid took pleasure in the act. He didn't. But Garod controlled him like he controlled every other to enter this arena. You fought and risked being killed or you refused and guaranteed your death.

Sauntering into the ring, the gray skinned Doorian stared straight ahead with his single eye. He was slender but muscled. Size wasn't an indicator of skill and the cyclops presence gave off a low vibration of warning. It would pay to be wary with this one. Garod had no idea what trouble he'd brought into his midst. Bommba stopped at the center, a few feet in front of Farid and the experienced group of fighters.

Garod called seven more names and each of the new contenders entered without restraints or struggle. To the casual observer, one would think them here by choice. Farid knew better. The conglomerate had ways of convincing its participants to fight. Very few were here willingly.

Family members, debt, criminal offenses and in some cases abduction—all of it was used to coerce individuals to fight without compensation.

"Next for your enjoyment, let's welcome, Zozo!" Garod yelled over the roaring crowd.

Farid gaped at the lumbering form entering the ring. Seven feet tall and well over one hundred and thirty five kilos, the horned male stood taller and broader than any other fighter Farid had ever faced. The audience went wild.

Manic glee glimmered from the gazes of those who watched the matches with relish and anticipation to the buyers who hoped to lease a new fighter. From the corner of his eyes, he caught Garod's smug grin. Farid's lips pressed tight. Garod could bring in fighters of all shapes and sizes. He didn't understand Farid was motivated by more than selfish greed and that same motivation would see him out of his *Gladyx* contract soon.

Garod waited until the volume lowered before speaking again. "That's all for now but check the holo vid updates on the screens in your room in a few days to see our other secret contenders. Fighters so out of control we couldn't bring them out today but you'll see live footage of them before anyone else. Then in action for their first premium edition matches!"

More screaming. Farid tuned it out and allowed his gaze to seek out the maintenance tech again. She stared directly at him. Reluctant desire returned with a vengeance. Farid immediately crushed the feeling. He'd gone too long without a female. That was all.

There was no room in his life for pleasure. But he couldn't look away from her.

***

None of the new fighters were cyborgs. Outwardly, Kelix retained his calm but it wasn't hard for Sora to sense his disappointment at not finding his missing pod brethren. Brows dipped low in a fierce frown, he turned to leave. "Excuse me."

"Of course." Sora stepped aside so he could get by her.

Waving at another buyer in the stands, Kelix eased around Sora. In a soft whisper, he said, "Update me as soon as you can. I want to know everything."

He didn't look back to see her response. Sora kept her eyes on the arena, watching as the fighters left the field. She would do some scouting to find out what she could about the new fighters and she knew exactly where to start.

Sora made her way out of the arena, blending with the streaming groups rushing for the exit. Chatter and excitement was in the air and Sora forced a smile to her lips, pretending to be as enraptured. Inside, fury rode her hard. Thinking of Zozo in his cage, alone, crying. The conglomerate and any affiliated with the actions of what took place on the *Gladyx* were going down if she had anything to say about it.

In the hall, Sora broke off from the crowd and headed to the lower deck and the maintenance department. The evening shift tended to be quiet and the same workers were always there. Two in particular Sora tried to befriend.

She tapped the door, pushed it open and feigned surprise. "Oh, I wasn't sure anyone was still here."

The startled faces eased and Kellina and Kaylen smiled at her. "Hey, Sora."

Sora came in and closed the door behind her then leaned back against the frame. Kellina and Kaylen were JAGS—joined at gestation siblings. For some reason in their race, the embryos occasionally merged in vitro and developed partly as one.

From what they'd told Sora, they functioned as separate individuals whenever possible despite sharing the main part of their body below the shoulders.

Kaylen on the left angled his head to see Sora and Kellina pushed their chair around to face her completely. "What are you doing here so late?"

Shrugging, Sora winked at Kaylen but answered Kellina, "I just left the new fighter introductions."

From the right side, Kellina nodded and smoothed back her hair. “Any cuties?”

Groaning, Kaylen smacked a palm to his face. “Don’t answer that.”

Sora laughed. “I may have noticed one or two attractive beings.”

Kelline raised her right hand and cheered while Kaylen tipped his head to the ceiling and shook it back and forth. “Why, Sora? Why did you tell her that?”

Chuckling at their antics, Sora straightened and moved from the door. “I had an urgent tech call from Dottie. She found me earlier and though I wasn’t on shift, she insisted I take the job.”

“On it.” Kellina spun the chair around and keyed up the reports. “I see it. She logged the call from Farid Ogoni and has you noted for the repair.”

Kaylen opened a separate holo screen on his end of the desk, left hand flying over the data. “Electrical work. Minor issue.”

He and Kellina glanced up at Sora but Kaylen spoke. “Should we close the order?”

“No. I told him I’d go back tomorrow and follow up. I needed a part to complete the job.” Which was a lie. She could easily destroy the listening device but Sora needed the excuse to return to his room in order to have a moment to talk with Farid alone.

Finding and destroying the listening device only increased the odds in her favor of getting him on her side.

Kaylen grimaced, his brown eyes going dark. “Simin will have a fit.”

Their boss loved to find small things to complain about as if they were huge issues however the dismay on the siblings' faces gave her an idea. "I was scheduled off today and didn't want to risk a flag in my file if he finds out I worked anyway."

"Hmm." Kellina met her brother's gaze and suddenly the two of them were typing quickly, swishing holo screens around and working their typical magic.

Sora didn't ask how they synchronized their body movements so seamlessly but each time she witnessed them working in one accord, she was impressed. Their dexterity and speed made them perfect as monitors for the call center in the maintenance department.

"Ha! Done," Kaylen announced.

"Damn it, brother. I was close," Kellina protested, slumping back in the chair.

Shaking her head, Sora waited. They turned their chair around and faced her. Kaylen wore a smug grin. "I created a temporary block window. It says you had two hours scheduled today to fill in for another tech who had a severe stomach issue. Simin won't think anything of it and it provides a good reason for why you worked on your day off. I even created a request for you to follow up."

Sora blew at kiss at them. "I love you both."

Kaylen flushed and Kellina reached over to ruffle his blond waves. "She doesn't mean it literally either."

"I *know* that." Kaylen glared at his sister. To Sora, he said, "You can stop in the supply closet on your way out to get the part. If it's a quick fix, you should be able to finish it today instead of tomorrow and Simin won't have room to complain about any changes on tomorrow's schedule."

"Done," Sora said.

She hurried to the closet, grabbed a random part and a repair kit to carry with her. While she wouldn't need anything in the kit, it would cover her using her abilities.

Chapter 6

Sora pounded on Farid's door with a determined knock. Shuffling from the other side assured he was inside and coming to answer. She scanned the hall to see if anyone watched or noted her presence outside his room with unusual attention. At this time of night, no one was around. Her shoulders eased a bit with the knowledge.

The door swung open and the man himself glared at her. Farid was still shirtless from the introduction show, only this time, he had a towel slung around his neck. "What are you doing back already?"

Gruff and with an edge of irritation, the question caught Sora off-guard and she found herself at a loss. After his heated stares in the arena, a small part of her had expected a more welcoming greeting. Straightening, she ignored the way his lashes curled over his hazel eyes and kept her voice to the point. "I came to fix your issue."

He braced one arm on the wall above his head, blocking her entry, then cocked his hip and leaned his weight forward. His voice was a rough rumble when he spoke. "You said tomorrow."

Right. Sora upped the wattage of her smile. "Yes, but I got approval to get the matter wrapped up tonight."

He continued to stare. Heat prickled her skin and Sora used her processors to lower her body's visible signs of embarrassment. Finally, when she was close to trying another tack, he eased back and pushed off the door, clearing the way for her to enter.

Taking a deep breath and releasing it slowly, she strolled in as if she didn't have a worry. The door closed with a definitive snap behind her as she headed to his bedroom.

Farid hovered near her and his presence set her nerves on edge. She pretended to retrieve the scanner from her bag and intentionally stumbled. Farid lost his glower to reach out and catch her by the arm.

"Careful."

"Thanks." She adjusted the bottom of her crop top which made no difference to its belly baring length but it had the benefit of drawing Farid's eyes. "I'll just take a look at the vid screen now."

He hadn't released his grip on her arm yet and his fingers tightened imperceptibly. "Is that wise?"

Again, she locked gazes with him. There was curiosity in his as well as suspicion. Always with the suspicion. Sora respected that. No one should trust anyone on this ship. "It's wise because I need to fix it. I only got approved to work a short period of time. I'm technically off today."

With a surprising gentleness she wouldn't have expected from one who spent his time fighting, his fingers caressed her skin then fell away. "Let's do it then."

It was as good as an agreement as she was going to get. Sora went right for the vid screen and swung it away from the wall. For the benefit of any ears listening, she said, "I should be able to switch out the imaging card and clear up the issue."

Leaning forward, she casually brushed her fingers over the small circular disc embedded in the wall and released a spark of energy. After a tiny fitz of sound, the blue dot blinked out. Sora sighed, dropping her pretense and straightened. "It's no longer transmitting."

The words were barely out of her mouth before Farid spun her around and slammed her against the wall beside the vid screen. He pressed his weight into hers, hands locked on her waist, holding her in place and snarled, "Who are you really and how did you know someone was listening to me?"

Sora remained loose and relaxed. Licking her lips, she return his glare for glare. "It's up to you whether you believe me or not, but I had no idea that was there. I came to fix one issue and *you* asked me to look at another. Remember?"

Sneering, Farid shook her then stepped back. "I don't trust you. Whatever you're up to, the answer is no. If you want me to throw a fight, no. If you want me to go after someone who rejected you, no."

Disbelief twisted Sora's mouth in a moue of disgust. "I can fight my own battles. I wouldn't need you to go after anyone for me."

Farid snorted and backed further away from her in a huff.

Sora moved from the wall and continued. "I didn't have anything to do with putting a listening device in your room. If I did, you wouldn't have found it easily nor would another tech."

His brows flew up and Sora took another step forward. Farid jerked the towel from his neck and tossed it to the floor. "Then you want me to throw a fight? I'm not surprised."

"Wrong again," she snapped. "I want your help to look for two friends. Xion and Kaito went missing and we received word that they were fighting onboard the *Gladyx*."

To Sora's surprise, he didn't immediately order her out. Puzzlement filled his gaze. "I don't know those names but I try not to get close to the other fighters so I can't help you."

"You can." She reached out imploringly. "Work with me and together we can search for them. Garod says he has more surprises in store for the guests onboard. It might be the two men I'm looking for."

She avoided mentioning they were cyborgs, not wanting to jeopardize the chance he believed the lies spreading about their kind.

Farid shifted his weight on his hips and crossed his arms over his chest. His green and brown patterned skin darkened. "What would I get out of doing this? In three days, my contract here is up. Why would I want to jeopardize that?"

She hadn't realized. Cyllus and Kelix knew nothing about this development. "What does that mean, 'your contract is up'? How does it work? The impression is that fighters fight until they die."

Farid lifted his shoulders in a dismissive gesture and went to sit on the edge of his bed. "Typically, but I made an agreement ten years ago and the conglomerate accepted."

There was more to it than that. Nothing was as simple as he made it seem when it came to the owners who ran the fight ring. Sora left his answer alone and pushed her point. "You can still help me. There's no way you don't realize something isn't right here. Work with me and we can help get you away from here."

He eyed her as if she'd lost her mind and maybe she had. Sora was desperate and this was the closest she'd gotten to any of the fighters.

"You seem to have missed my point. I don't need your help. With the fight schedule as it stands, I'll be done in a matter of days and can walk away free and clear."

Sora bit back an expletive. If that was the case, he was right. Appealing to his nature would obviously be a waste too. Truth be told, in his position, Sora couldn't say if she'd risk her freedom for a stranger either. "At least tell me how they get so many fighters to stay. What loyalty drives you?"

His hooded gaze locked on her. "The thrill. The credits. It's a rush."

Lie. She didn't get an adrenalin seeker vibe from him. Sora planted her hands on her hips at the blatant untruth he'd just tried to blow her off with. "What about the death matches? You're telling me they stay here and risk death because of a thrill?"

It didn't seem feasible. Farid stayed separate from the others, he fought with a thirst and level of aggression she'd only witnessed when someone's life was on the line. Sora would know since her escape from the emperor had been that way.

"I'm telling you it's none of your business."

The flat statement was spoken without inflection but Sora took note of the stiff way he held himself on the bed. "You're fine with fighters being forced to be here?"

He arched a single brow and cocked his head to the side. "*Are* they being forced?"

Damn him. He didn't have to answer though. The truth sat right in front of her. There was no way a man as strong and skilled as Farid Ogoni wanted to be here, spending his time fighting match after match. It didn't make any more sense now then it did when they'd compiled their reports on all of the fighters.

"You have an undefeated record of 543-0. If you wanted, you could beat them, fight your way out. Are they holding something against you?"

The more Sora thought on it, the more the belief solidified that he was here against his will.

Farid's gaze hardened and the sardonic amusement he'd viewed her with faded. "I think we can both agree it's time for you to leave."

That was as good as a *get the fuck out* as she'd ever heard. If Sora tried to push harder, she'd get nowhere. Time to bow out gracefully and regroup later.

"I understand. Thank you anyway for listening. As to the device, your vid screen should work fine now. It's shorted out. That doesn't mean they won't replace it. Maybe somewhere less obvious but if things work out the way you expect, it won't matter because you'll soon be gone."

"Exactly." He stood and gestured to the hall. "I'll walk you out. Good luck with your search for your friends."

"Yeah," she muttered.

He wisely didn't comment on her disgruntled tone. They made their way down the hall, pass the kitchen and living room then stopped at the door. Sora hoped he'd say something else, make a counter offer of help but he waited for her to open the door and closed it behind her without saying bye.

***

Farid admitted it had been hard to resist Sora's plea. The darkened gaze and pink cheeks during her impassioned speech sparked a need in him. Her pretty eyes made him want to give her whatever she wanted. Every word she spoke came too close to finding out his secret.

Knowing someone else sought the truth and wanted to take action tempted him. It was almost a physical ache refusing her. He sighed. The risk was too great and he couldn't take the chance of angering the members of the conglomerate.

The fact that she searched for her friends and wasn't simply stalking him went a long way to lowering his concern regarding her purpose in appearing where he was twice in a row. He didn't believe in coincidences and as a new tech onboard, he'd noted her presence. Farid noticed *every* new crew member's presence.

Now he had an answer to his previous suspicions that she was a spy planted by Garod to lure him into staying. It wouldn't be the first time that happened.

His comm buzzed and thoughts of the slender, but curved brunette vanished. Farid hurried to his comm and answered. "Hello?"

"I thought you'd like an update. It's been a little bit."

Garod's gloating voice rubbed against Farid's skin like an abrasive brush. *A little bit*. It had been months since the last report but Farid knew better than to bring that point up. At every opportunity, if given the chance, Garod loved to play games with Farid's emotions.

"I'd like that," he said simply.

"Of course, if you sign for another year, I could convince the other members to agree to overnight stays starting tonight in fact," Garod offered.

"No." Farid clenched his free hand at his side and exhaled softly. This wasn't the first time. Garod had made similar offers in the past few months. The payoff wasn't worth it. He had to tell himself that over and over as his heart longed to accept.

Three days. Two wins. That's all Farid had left. He only had to hold out and all of this would be behind him.

"Thank you," he tacked on belatedly in case Garod used that as an excuse to skip the update he dangled.

Garod sighed overly loud. "You're missing out. The fans love you."

Farid pressed his lips tight and held his silence.

Another sigh. "Here's the report. He grew another inch in height and his frame is filling out. The claws developing last year have fully grown in. Speech and motor skills are fine and on track."

As he listened to Garod rattle off a few more dry stats, Farid gripped the comm tight. His heart pounded with each word. He sucked the details in with a hunger he could never contain during one of these comms. Garod knew that and doled them out in tiny bite sized increments.

"That's all it says," Garod finished.

Farid closed his eyes and tipped his head back. He forced himself to speak the gratitude he hated giving. "Thanks, Garod."

"We could give Turin a great legacy if you stick around," Garod tried again.

Opening his eyes, Farid gritted out, "My son's only legacy will be a life of freedom with his father."

Chapter 7

Making comm calls required care and planning. Sora checked her room for visual or listening devices. Finding one in Farid's place made her more cautious. If the powers that be kept their top fighter under surveillance, it wasn't a stretch to imagine they did it to others.

Her scanners didn't pick up anything and as a cyborg she had top tech implanted in her head and trusted her sensors. Assured she was as safe as possible, she knelt on the floor and eased back a section of the tiling. Reaching inside, she removed her personal comm and sat back on her heels.

No messages but she didn't expect any. She and Kelix were extremely cautious in the contact they made with their friends or anyone who could have the conglomerate members suspect they weren't who they claimed.

Sora thought over Farid's rejection last night. Without his help, she was no closer to finding out or getting near a fighter for the truth. She and Kelix would have to up their efforts. She flicked her thumb over the familiar ID code.

"Hey, Sora!"

Savannah's bright voice brought a reluctant smile to Sora's face. The human female from the newest planet in the Protectorate had a way about her. "Hey, Savie. Is Cyllus around?"

"I'm here," came a deeper masculine tone.

"I'm waiting to see if Kelix joins us," Sora started. "How's...how's Thalen?"

"Good," Savie chirped. "We're in Tagan's rooms now, visiting. Have a look."

A miniature holo image suddenly appeared as Savie switched the device from audio to visual. The tiny figure of Savie surrounded by a blue glow was a welcome sight. Sora had grown to care for the human from Earth.

Savie leaned to the side and the view changed. Behind her, lying in bed, a large male slept, unaware. His sharp features were relaxed in repose. Someone had trimmed his hair and it lay in neat waves about his head.

The severe bruising on his face had faded but burn scars were still visible on his throat and the upper portion of his chest and shoulders. Sora swallowed and lifted a hand to hover in the air. "Thalen."

Her choked whisper caught her off guard. She thought she'd dealt with her emotions seeing Thalen like this. She was beyond thankful he'd survived but the pain of him in this state stabbed at her heart. They weren't just pod mates. Thalen was the closest thing Sora had to a brother.

"How is he?" she asked.

Tagan's face appeared next to Thalen's. "He's recovering. His nanobots are back to operating at peak efficiency."

Though Tagan spoke in a cold, firm voice, Sora trusted the other cyborg. He'd promised to take care of Thalen while she took this mission with Kelix and he'd not let her down yet.

"The burns?"

Thalen had been severely injured a little over a month ago. He should have died from the internal and external damage he'd sustained but he'd found shelter with a local woman on

Solus and she'd hidden him from potential exposure and being recaptured by Emperor Shui.

Tagan's gaze narrowed. "At this rate, there will be scarring."

Sora nodded, swallowing past the lump in her throat. She'd expected such. It wasn't a big deal in comparison to his life. Thalen wasn't vain. His looks and the burn scars wouldn't hinder him living a full life. If he would just wake up. There was no reason for him to still be in repair mode.

"Thanks for looking after him, Tagan." She meant it sincerely.

"What about us?" Cyllus asked.

A snort laugh bubbled up, dispelling Sora's sadness about her friend's condition. "Thank you, all."

Two taps at the door interrupted what she'd been about to say. "I think that's Kelix."

Sora flipped the comm face down in case it wasn't and went to the door. A thermal scan beyond the barrier reflected a single figure standing on the other side. She opened it and Kelix quickly came in.

"I have Cyllus and the others on comm," Sora spoke as she went to retrieve the device.

Together they viewed the small holo image of Cyllus. The casual smile he'd worn when he spoke to Sora expanded to a larger grin and his gaze brightened. "Greetings, Kelix."

"You as well, Cyllus." The slight smile Kelix wore was as warm as Sora ever saw but then Cyllus and Kelix were pod brethren and close friends from their younger years. Kelix faced her. "Tell us what you've learned."

She explained finding the listening device in Farid's room on a maintenance call and his reaction.

"Did he say who put it there? Does he have an idea?" Kelix pressed eagerly.

Sora shook her head and drove her fingers through her hair. "His contract will be up if he wins his last two fights so he didn't much seem to care."

"I've never heard of someone getting out or finishing a contract," Cyllus mused.

It was news to Sora too but nothing in her auditory senses hinted at Farid's statement being a lie.

"Unless, they lied to him." Kelix's speculation sounded more accurate and in line with her thoughts.

"There's also the chance they're blackmailing him," Cyllus added.

Sora tapped a finger against her thigh and ran through probable scenarios. "If that's the case, it explains why he wouldn't want to work with us. What could they possibly have on him for ten years? That's a long time."

"Crimes?" Kelix muttered. "Maybe they have knowledge of crimes he committed and are holding it over his head."

True. And they would know. Sora fingered the prosthetic covering the CR brand on her cheek. Cyborgs had followed orders and been labeled traitors to their world. After receiving a life sentence for their rebellious actions, they were loaded up on a transport ship bound for a prison moon.

"It explains the other fighters never leaving if they're being blackmailed."

From the stories told, the conglomerate had earned their reputation for being cruel and vicious. Unfortunately, Kelix and Sora hadn't caught sight of anything to prove it nor had they managed to speak to a single fighter directly without others around.

Crossing paths with Farid and speaking to him had been pure chance. Getting inside the lower levels to the fighters yesterday had been a stroke of luck and the closest Sora had managed to get. She couldn't count on that happening again.

"Is there anyway we can convince or sway this Farid to our side?" Cyllus asked.

Kelix tipped his head toward Sora. "I think there's an attraction for Sora there. We could exploit it."

Heat seared Sora's cheeks as Cyllus' gaze shifted toward her. She cleared her throat. "If there is an attraction, he's not acting on it. When I left his room last night, he made it clear he wasn't open to helping. He's only thinking of his two remaining fights and leaving."

Kelix grunted. "He's confident he'll win which means he's not worried and believes whatever promises they made. I almost feel sorry for him if he thinks they'll actually let him leave so easily. Farid's one of their biggest draws for revenue."

Stiffening, Sora studied Kelix's face. "What are you thinking?"

His mouth twisted and his brows drew low in the middle. "I've talked to the other buyers. He's a hot commodity in demand. I'd be willing to wager the conglomerate will do something to extend his time. Anything.

"Despite what he's saying about a contract, I can't find a single record of any fighter *ever* leaving except as a dead body."

Sora cursed. Kelix was right. They'd done their research and run as many reports as possible before undertaking this mission. No fighter left the *Gladyx* alive.

Cyllus sighed, pulling her attention back to him. "Part of me wants Kaito and Xion to be there so we can bring them home but the other part of me is scared of what condition we'll find them in if they are there. Sora, do whatever you can to get close to Farid. Kelix, find what the conglomerate have on him. There has to be a way to get his help. He's our only lead at this point."

***

Rage filled his blood as Farid viewed the update with the information regarding his fight schedule. Garod wanted to play games. According to the display, there was no match listed for Farid. He growled low in his throat. Not today, not tomorrow. Almost shaking with his fury, he stabbed his fingers on his comm.

Garod answered on the first trill. His holo image sat on a lounge, holding a drink aloft in his hand. "Farid, what a surprise."

The gloating greeting sent Farid's anger soaring higher. His muscles flexed and burned with the need to act. Taking several deep breaths, Farid regained control of his emotions enough to ask. "I had two fights listed this week and now they're gone."

"Hmm." Garod's lips pursed as if in thought. Then he snapped his fingers. "Yes, I remember now. We have the new fighters and everyone's eager to see them in action. We had to make changes."

Farid cautioned himself to stay calm. He knew exactly what Garod sought to do and if Farid gave in to his anger, the conversation would lead nowhere. "When is my next fight?"

Garod tsked, his voice somber as he said, "I'm not sure. You know how these things go, Farid. We cater to you when possible because you've been such a good source of revenue and a crowd pleaser. With you leaving, we have to focus on our other talent. Build up the excitement around them to make up for your loss."

"I need those two fights," Farid gritted out, jamming a hand through his unbound hair. "You promised. Breaking the contract makes my obligation to you null and void. I can take Turin and leave."

Laughter met his threat. Garod set his drink down out of sight of the screen and leaned forward in his seat. "No one's breaking the contract, Farid. After you win your last two bouts, you'll be free to take your son and leave."

"Then schedule them!" The outburst escaped his control as Farid began to pace the length of his living room. He needed to fight. He needed this living nightmare to be over. He wasn't sure how much longer he could hold on. So many things hinged on Farid winning and finally being able to leave.

Garod's tone darkened and the spikes on his neck quivered. "I don't work for you, Farid Ogoni. You work for *me* and need to remember that. Turin isn't going anywhere and neither are you if I have anything to say about it."

The comm ended, leaving dead air and static from the holo behind. Farid roared and flung the device across the room. It hit the wall and dropped to the floor with a clatter. He should have expected something like this. Farid stormed back and forth. Why did he think it would be easy?

Nothing when dealing with the conglomerate was easy. How many times had he watched fighters carried out of the arena in death bags? How many of them had he placed there?

His fingers clenched. He'd grown cocky. Without those two fights, he could be held here indefinitely. He'd assumed the conglomerate would want him to fight in order to rake in the credits since he'd be gone soon. He wasn't stupid. His fights were huge profit generators.

If Garod and the others were willing to forego Farid's matches what else would they do to hold him here? What if they didn't release his son as they'd promised?

Ten years he'd patiently waited. Ten years of wondering, waiting. And all because of Ashme. Turin's mother had been a female fighter in the arenas before him. Farid had been ensnared by her beauty during a visit with fellow Gurzals to watch a fight. They'd drank, partied and made bad decisions the entire week they were onboard.

Bad decisions. Farid snorted and stopped in the middle of the room, forcing his breathing to settle. Ashme seduced him to her bed with flirty smiles and hot kisses. The next morning when Farid planned to leave with his friends at the space station, she'd cried pretty tears and begged Farid to take her with him.

He'd refused, of course. Then two days later, still hanging with his friends at the space station, he'd received a message from Ashme saying she carried his child from their night together.

The possibility was slim but he'd owed it to himself to confirm. Gurzals could scent pregnancy. Like a fool, Farid sent his friends on their way, promising to join them later at the next station stop. He'd returned to the *Gladyx* alone. As soon as he met Ashme in her rooms, he'd scented the pregnancy.

She'd already had a medic report run and the genetic data proved he was the father. Then Ashme pleaded with Farid to save her and their child. She'd gripped his hand tightly in hers and stared into his eyes. "Even if you don't want me. We don't have to be together, Farid, but our child doesn't deserve this. They'll keep it."

That's when Farid made another mistake. He met with Garod and the other two members of the conglomerate in hopes of bargaining for Ashme's release and that of his child.

At first, Garod had been full of understanding at Farid's position. He smiled and leaned back in his chair, with his right leg crossed over the knee of his left. "Obviously the unborn baby isn't ours. But, Ashme made a commitment to us and we can't simply let her go. If we break the rules for one, we'd have fighters all over looking for ways to get out."

"Isn't there anything you can do? I'll take the child. Ashme's already decided she doesn't want to be a mother and is willing to cede legal guardianship to me as the father."

What a fool, Farid had been. The moment he'd said those words and revealed his position, he'd sealed his fate.

Garod's gaze grew intent. He dropped his leg to the floor and leaned forward. "There is something you can do. A deal we can work out and we'll release Ashme the moment she gives birth."

Thinking only of the fate of his child, Farid blurted. "I'll do it. Whatever it takes."

Farid spent the next ten years regretting those words although he didn't regret his son. On his darkest days, Turin was his motivation to win and not give up.

Like agreed, the conglomerate let Ashme go the day after she gave birth. Without a single glance at the baby she'd delivered, she'd waved at Farid with a backpack slung over her shoulder and marched jauntily off the *Gladyx* at the next available station.

Leaving Farid behind, bound to a ten year contract to fight in her place and a new baby to care for.

Ten years and five hundred and forty-five fights. That's what had been decreed in the documents Farid signed. At the time, he'd thought it would be easy enough to accomplish. How naïve. Every match, every death, every port, he'd counted down the number of fights. It took a toll but he'd held firm and kept his mind on the end prize. Freedom. Farid had met the ten year mark a month ago.

And now he was at five hundred and forty-three. Two more to go. But if Garod had his way, there'd never be a five hundred and forty-five for Farid, leaving him forever in limbo and trapped.

His son didn't deserve this life. Turin had known nothing but imprisonment on a ship. From the moment of birth, Garod assured Farid his son would be with a caretaker who adored Turin. He'd met the woman when Turin was a week old and Farid entered his first fight. She'd seemed agreeable enough and he had to believe nothing had changed in all that time.

In the early days, Garod allowed Farid to see his son once a week. He'd lived for those moments. Sometimes it was all he had to cling to when his body hurt, his bones were broken and his eyes were so swollen he couldn't see. Being with his son on that single day made it worth it.

Until Turin's fifth year and the visits came to an abrupt end.

"The boy is getting older and parting from you upsets him. It takes a lot for the caretaker to settle him. It's best we limit the contact with you," Garod announced the first time Farid had been blocked from his son's room.

Farid had tossed a desk through a wall in Garod's office. Nothing had changed the decree. In an instant, one man's command kept Farid from visitation with his son.

No yelling, no fighting, no begging—Farid choked on the memory. He'd gotten on his knees and begged Garod not to end the visits. It hadn't mattered.

And here Farid was, relegated to verbal second hand updates on the condition of his son. It was almost over though. Farid had made Turin a promise when he was little, one he planned to stand by. They would both walk off this ship together or no one on the *Gladyx* would survive the devastation Farid wreaked in his wake.

Chapter 8

"A son!" Sora burst out as soon as she and Kelix met in an empty cleansing room the next day. She locked the door behind her and crossed the space to Kelix, excitement bubbling beneath the surface.

Kelix gaped. "A son?"

"Farid has a son. They're using him to keep Farid fighting."

Kelix's black eyes gleamed. "We can use this. Tell me everything."

"I was outside his room with the intent to see if I could play on the attraction between us. I picked up the sound of voices inside and listened through the door. Garod has Farid's son and the two of them will be free once Farid wins two more fights. Garod changed the schedule and there are no fights for Farid this week."

Kelix's gaze widened. "That's beyond cruel. Without the fights, Farid's trapped here."

Sora agreed. It was cruel and intentional.

"This means we have something to work with and can get him on our side," Kelix continued.

Sora bit her inner cheek. She didn't like the idea of using Farid's son against him. Even for their cause. Children were innocent.

"Sora?"

Swiping a hand through her hair, Sora nodded. "Right. Sorry. I just...the idea of this child caught in the middle doesn't sit well with me."

A moment passed then Kelix blew out a breath and cursed. "Agreed. I got caught up in wanting a way to find my pod mates. Using a child makes me no better than Garod."

"I'm on duty so I can't stay long. I'll see if I can find where Garod's holding the child. If we can get him out of here, it will free Farid up to make a decision without worry."

Kelix nodded. "Do it."

Sora unlocked the door and looked both ways. The hall was clear. She eased out and headed down the hall. She needed to find out what she could about Farid's son and where he was being kept.

The search would be easier if she could access her mainframe and sort through all the data available in the ship's computer. That wasn't possible though because Emperor Shui had hacked the cyborg mainframe when he discovered their rebel plans to stop his efforts to take over the neighboring planet Bionus.

Now like all cyborgs, Sora did her best to stay offline outside of what her neural net processor could do.

"Sora!" Dottie crouched in the hall screwing in an electro panel. "How did everything go the other day? Was Simin mad about the off-shift hours?"

Sora stopped beside her. "No. Everything was fine."

Wiggling her eyebrows, Dottie dusted her hands off and packed her tools. "What about Farid Ogoni? Is he as sexy close up?"

Laughing, Sora dodged the question. "Are you done for the day?"

"I have a few more tickets left before I can log out. Why?"

Sora lifted her shoulder casually as Dottie stood. "Just wondering."

Dottie smiled. Sora had learned that those who worked on the *Gladyx* didn't ask questions. They accepted everything at face value. Or rather they preferred to turn a blind eye to the things going on around them. Dottie liked to chat and share whatever she knew. The tech had no filter.

"Where are you headed?" Dottie asked, picking up her tool kit box.

"I have a full schedule and several repairs to see to. A few on this level then the lower deck."

Dottie bumped her hip into Sora's. "Are you hoping to run into a certain fighter?"

Sora winked and let the other tech make of it what she would. Keeping her tone, even, Sora wondered aloud, "I don't see a lot of kids around. We get so many travelers on and off, I expected to run into a couple."

As if by mutual agreement, they started down the hall together, Dottie swinging her kit back and forth. "Oh, there are a few. Javi in maintenance has a little girl but she stays in the care center while she works. Ren also has kids but he's in security and has trust issues so they stay in his room with an approved caretaker."

This was news to Sora and a potential starting point. She hadn't even considered the children aspect. "I didn't know there was a care center on board."

"Sure. The workers who have kids have to have someone to watch them. It's on the lower deck, toward the back. I like to go there on bad days and watch them playing through the screen," Dottie said, unaware she'd revealed something important.

"Can anyone go? I mean...I would think as a safety measure, visits would be limited to family."

Dottie waved her hand dismissively in the air. "Meh. Once I tell them I'm in maintenance, they don't say anything. Children break things all the time, so I fix a gadget or two while there and no one reports me."

"Interesting," Sora murmured as a plan began to form. "I'll see you later. Don't want to hold you up."

"See you, Sora." Dottie skipped off, bopping her head.

At the divide in the corridor, Dottie went right and Sora made a sharp left. She took the ladder to the lower level, not wanting to wait for the lift. On the bottom rung, Sora jumped to the floor and brushed the grit from her hands as she glanced around. The hum of machinery broke the almost silent hall.

According to her memory, the engineering and security team worked down here too. A tour hadn't been part of the hiring process so this was her first time in this section.

The majority of the *Gladyx*'s central computer functions routed through this area. Having the care center in a location with minimum traffic was smart thinking. No one would wander to this section unless they needed to be here.

Shoulders back and head up, Sora kept her arms loose at her sides and strolled down the hall as if she belonged. Only a handful of crew in uniform passed her and they barely made eye contact. Maybe because she wore the distinct gray jumpsuit for the maintenance department.

Whatever the reason, Sora was grateful it allowed her to walk through unchallenged. Childish giggles reached her from up ahead as she approached a room. Her steps slowed and Sora waited for someone to yell out or ask her questions.

She reached the opened door and peered inside. Children ran and played on colorful structures placed throughout the large room. Drones whirled in the air near the ceiling, chirping instructions.

"Walk, do not run. Play safe. Sharing is caring."

Two adults stood like smiling sentinels along one wall, the other wall consisted of a giant window. Probably the one Dottie used when she viewed the children.

"Can I help you?" a soft voice asked from behind.

She'd heard the slivering steps but pretended to be caught unaware and turned. "Oh. Hello."

The Cepphi female balanced easily on her tentacled limbs. She wore a loose purple smock that hung on her lean frame. Kind eyes gazed at Sora as she waited for a response.

Going with a partial truth, Sora pasted a smile on her face. "I'm surprising a friend and thought I'd check in on his child first. It's been a while since I've seen either of them and thought to get a quick peek in between my shift."

The Cepphi extended her hand and waved at the room of playing children. "Secured cameras run a live feed throughout the day for parents, family and friends to view the children at any time. If you have the access code, you can see them whenever you want on a vid screen in your room."

Sora thought quickly and faked a laugh. "Oh. He didn't mention that. This is why surprises don't work."

She turned as if to leave but the woman stopped her. "Which child are you looking for?"

What was the child's name? There had been a name mentioned during Farid's comm. Sora flipped through her memory files and found it. "Turin. He was very young the last time I saw him and might not remember me."

The woman's smile fell and her blue eyes dimmed. "Oh, this is awkward. I'm sorry to be the one to tell you—Turin died."

Sora's stomach dropped. "W-what?"

Sympathy glimmered from the other woman's gaze. "Five years ago, he got ill. Garod had Turin rushed to the medical facility and two days later we were informed young Turin wouldn't return and hadn't survived his illness. Chala, his caretaker, was let go soon after."

Did Farid know? Of course he didn't, she instantly castigated herself. He wouldn't still be fighting on the *Gladyx*, wouldn't have turned Sora down. Farid believed his son still lived and planned to take him away when he finishing fighting. He'd implied as much without revealing he had a child.

Sora gasped. This was why Garod changed Farid's fight schedule. He *couldn't* let the contract be completed because the child, his bargaining chip, no longer lived.

Farid! She had to tell him. Sora squeezed the woman's shoulder. "Thank you for letting me know before I did something insensitive and mentioned the child to my friend."

"I really am sorry to ruin your surprise. Turin was a delight to all of us. Bright, sweet and full of such energy."

"Thank you." Sora hurried down the hall, her only thought to get to Farid and tell him what the conglomerate had been hiding. He deserved to know. She couldn't imagine how this news would affect him.

***

Farid wasn't in the mood for the knock that came at his door. He opened it a crack and glared at the maintenance tech. "I don't have any repair tickets on file."

Her gaze widened in surprise at his appearance and he didn't have to wonder why. Farid had been drinking in frustration about Garod rearranging his fight schedule. Thinking of how this delayed his ability to take Turin and leave set him off and now he didn't want to deal with anyone.

"I was hoping to talk," she said solemnly.

"Go away," he growled.

When he tried to slam the door shut, she grabbed the jamb. Farid pushed, intending to block her from entering and met resistance.

To his surprise, the frame barely budged despite the pressure he added. His gaze widened and he met her even stare.

"You're going to want to let me in," she stated quietly.

He gave one more determined push but there was no sign of strain on her face as she held the door easily in her tight grip. He eyed her from head to toe in the gray uniform and boots.

Slight of weight, he should be able to crush her with the amount of pressure, he exerted on the door. Maybe the alcohol had impaired him more than he thought. "How are you doing this?"

"That's part of what we can also talk about."

He could have forced the issue but his curiosity won out over his anger. He also lacked a desire to hurt her by forcing the issue. Giving in, Farid stepped aside.

Sora immediately came in, closing the door behind her. "Thank you."

He snorted and arched a brow. "Don't thank me. It wasn't by choice. Start talking."

She offered a rueful shrug but something about her manner was off. The few times they'd spoken before, Sora had been determined but with a lighter air about her. Now, the angle of her shoulders reflected a stiff resolve and her eyes held a dark glimmer of remorse.

An uncomfortable sensation rolled over Farid, dimming the hazy effect of the liquor he'd consumed. "What is it?"

She drew a deep breath and exhaled softly. "When was the last time you saw your child?"

Farid stilled, then his heart jumped in his chest. He reached out and grabbed her uniform at the chest area, yanking her up on her toes. "What do you know of Turin?"

Sora didn't struggle, remaining limp in his hold. Her unwavering stare held his gaze. "I came to talk to you earlier and heard you mention a son."

His lips curled in a snarl. "If you think to hurt—"

"Never!" she spat, knocking his hand away. The move stunned Farid enough to release her. She balanced easily on her feet and adjusted her rumpled clothing. "I would never harm a child."

"Then why are you asking about my son?" Trust was a commodity Farid didn't extend to anyone associated with the *Gladyx* and as far as he was concerned, Sora was aligned with them.

"Listen to me carefully, Farid. I need you to answer and I'll tell you everything you want to know. Can you tell me the last time you *actually* saw your son?"

Unexpected worry caused him to hesitate. Had something happened to Turin? Blood pumped through his veins on a surge as a low thrum of fear unfurled. "It's been a few years but I get reports from Garod."

"What kind of reports?"

"Forget the reports!" he roared on another shot of adrenalin. "Tell me what this is about or leave."

"I spoke to a woman working in the children's care center and she said Turin is...dead."

"No." Farid backed away from her and the words she spoke. His vision blurred and tunneled. "No, you're wrong. The worker is wrong."

His son wasn't dead.

Sympathy pierced Sora's gaze. "She said Turin got ill."

Illness he could deal with. Turin was strong. Gurzals hardly ever sickened. Farid turned for the door. "Is he in the medical center?"

She grabbed his arm and he shook her off of him. "Don't touch me! I need to go to my son."

He stormed for the door when Sora called out, "He died five years ago, Farid. I'm so sorry to have to tell you that."

Chapter 9

Sora had gone through a lot of difficult things in life, her experience with Emperor Shui not withstanding. Nothing came close to the look of devastation on Farid's face when she told him his son was dead. Her heart ached for him.

Farid spun around and pointed at her accusingly. Pain twisted his features into a mask of grief and anger. "You're lying! You're only saying this to get me to work with you to find your friends. Get out!"

Sora flinched and took a step toward him. She kept her arms out to her side and tried to calm him. "I can't imagine what you're feeling right now but I wouldn't lie about that. I have no reason to lie but think about who does. Who would want to keep that information away from you, Farid?"

As he moved away from the door, his chest rose and fell with each jagged inhale. His hazel eyes dimmed to a light shade of brown as he struggled to make sense of what she'd told him. Sora fought the urge to wrap her arms around him.

Emotions had become a distant thing for her. Part of converting to a cyborg during her military service meant having a portion of her organic brain merged with a cybernetic processor. In essence, sacrificing one thing gave her the ability to access a wide range of information with a simple thought.

Right now, Sora could use a bit of that disconnect. She hurt on Farid's behalf. She hurt for the loss he'd suffered and the pain Garod's lies had caused. No one deserved to learn of their child's death years after the fact. And no one deserved hearing that news from a stranger.

Farid turned further away from the door and approached her with heavy strides, his expression dark with pain and anger. "Are you telling me Garod lied to me? For *five* years?"

Sora laced her fingers together in front of her and nodded. If nothing else, she intended to make sure when this was over, Garod suffered. She'd do the deed herself and rip his head from his shoulders. Nothing else would do for this blatant act of cruelty.

Farid's chest heaved and he shuddered as he stumbled toward the sofa and crashed down on it. Unsure what to do, Sora remained standing and waited. A keening sound came from deep in his chest, broken only by a harsh sob. Shoulders shaking, he buried his face in his hands.

Sora cursed and crossed to the sofa, dropping to sit next to him. Her hands hovered awkwardly in the air until she gave in and wrapped them about his shoulders.

His despair was heart wrenching. Stars! She tugged him in closer. Initially, he resisted then his body gave way and melted against her. She held him as tight as she could. The way she'd wanted someone to hold her when she'd lost her family.

Aside from that initial sound, Farid was a silent crier but as he grew still, sorrow continued to emanate from him. The quiet way he held his body scraped against her nerves. She'd prefer he scream, curse. Anything but this deadly silence.

After a few moments of the unnerving quiet, she said, "He'll pay, Farid. I can do it tonight. Say the word and Garod will be dead before morning."

As soon as she uttered the vow, Sora knew she meant it. She'd jeopardize the mission, possibly ruin the chance for Kelix and Cyllus to find the missing members of their pod, if Farid rightly demanded justice.

"What are you?" He leaned up and away when he asked the question and slouched against the back of the sofa, eyeing her. Every line of his body appeared etched with weariness, his eyes more green now and red rimmed.

Sora swallowed. "I'm taking a chance on what I'm about to admit but I don't think you'll care."

He didn't speak.

Under his steady regard, Sora had an attack of nerves. Suppressing the sensation with an absentminded thought to her processors, she angled her legs to the side and reached up to carefully peel back the prosthetic cheek coverings she wore. Face bare, she looked into his eyes and declared, "I'm a cyborg."

Farid's gaze went straight to the crude CR brand on her face.

"I'm wanted for treason on my world, Kirs. The emperor has an alert out for the capture of any and all cyborgs convicted of launching a rebellion against him," she continued.

"The friends you're looking for, they're cyborgs too?" His voice came out a low rasp.

Her response was a tight nod. At this point, offering the information wouldn't damage their cause too much since she was sure the conglomerate knew who they held in their cages.

"Are you..." Farid cleared his throat. "Are you sure about...Turin?"

The slim thread of hope in the question gutted Sora. Her heart sank at not being able to tell him what he wanted. "I wish I was mistaken in what I heard."

"I'm going to kill him." After making that calm statement, Farid launched to his feet and headed for the door.

Sora beat him there and plastered her body in front of it. "Think, Farid. Garod has guards. There's high level security around the section of the cruiser housing each member of the conglomerate."

He stopped directly in front of her. "I don't know much about cyborgs but I assume if you wanted, you could bypass all of that. Help me get to Garod and I'll help you find your friends."

This was what Cyllus and Kelix wanted except no way could Sora take advantage of his grief. "I offered to kill him for you and I meant it but if Garod is to pay, all of the members in the conglomerate need to be taken down and the *Gladyx* put out of commission. If we go after him now, there's no guarantee the others won't get away."

"What do you suggest, Sora? That I let him live after he knowingly kept my son's death from me?" Farid's voice cracked on the last words and his eyes blazed with a mix of unchecked fury and such agony she could barely stand to witness it.

"Work with me and we'll take them all down. Garod and the others will pay for Turin and all the innocents they've harmed with their actions."

He sighed, gripped the back of his neck then said, "What do you need me to do?"

Sora breathed a sigh of relief at his reasonable tone. "I need to get in to see the new fighters."

"Impossible," he said in an instant.

"What? But I got in the other day."

His gaze widened. "How?"

"A guard. He mistook my presence for a repair order I think." She hiked a shoulder. "I was able to get in the lower levels behind the arena but only saw a few of the new fighters."

"He's dead."

"What?!" she had no idea what he was referencing.

Farid cracked his knuckles and crossed his arms over his chest. "There are security cams and surveillance all over that area. If a guard let you in, mistake or not, he was dead the moment his shift ended. It's what happens whenever an unapproved guest, crew member or visitor makes it to the back."

Every word he spoke rang with truth. Sora cringed inwardly. She hadn't meant to get the naïve guard killed. Still. "What about me? No ones said anything to me."

"It will probably be assumed that you were working. Except there's a separate maintenance crew for anything pertaining to the fight cages so consider yourself on their watch list at this point. As to guests or those who manage to see what the conglomerate wants kept secret, their disappearances are generally ignored."

Sora cursed. "I need to know if Kaito and Xion are here."

"I'll look. I'm not scheduled to fight this week but no one would think anything of me going to view my competition."

Based on his behavior in the past, she knew for a fact it wasn't something he did. "That's too risky, Farid."

Anger flashed, momentarily covering the sadness swamping his eyes. "Nothing matters to me anymore, Sora. Turin was my reason for pushing through the last ten years. Without him..."

***

Farid broke off what he'd been saying. There wasn't anything more to add. He didn't know what else to say or do. He'd gone from one extreme with Garod changing his schedule to keep him onboard to...to this devastating news. How could—how could his son be dead?

It didn't seem possible. None of this did. The alcohol he'd drunk earlier wasn't helping. His heart lay in his chest like a million fragments. Thinking of little Turin ripped him to pieces and Farid knew his soul would never be the same. All of these years, all of this time, and Garod had *lied*.

His son was gone and it didn't matter if he had one more fight or a hundred scheduled. He and Turin would never be together. Never have a chance to finally live together as a family. Farid had failed the one person who mattered and counted on him.

Nothing could assuage the grief in his spirit. Rage coalesced into a tight ball at the center of his gut. But he could try to forget. He stared at the maintenance tech. With this woman, he could block the pain and forget for a little time.

"Are you alright?" Sora asked.

"No," he admitted honestly, closing the distance between them. "I'm not."

Farid wasn't sure what was on his mind when he slid his hands up and down Sora's bare arms, only that he wanted—no, needed a distraction from the flow of pain shredding him. He leaned in to kiss Sora and she ducked. "Whoa. Wait."

He walked her backward. "Why wait?"

Her lids fluttered and she continued her backward trek. "You're emotional. Not thinking."

There were plenty of thoughts in his head but he only wanted to focus on one. Sora unerringly went down the hall and stopped at his bedroom door. Right where he wanted her. Farid picked her up and headed for the massive bed taking up most of the space. He tumbled them onto the bed and landed on top of her.

"I want to fuck you," he muttered, pulling back enough to stare into her eyes.

Blinking into his face, she paused. Farid knew his words had been stark in their simplicity and waited. She stared and said, "I think I picked up on that."

"This isn't special. This isn't anything more," he continued as if he needed to drive home the point. "I don't have more to offer anyone. I want a raw fuck to deal with the fury burning inside of me. Do you understand what I'm saying, Sora?"

She drove her finger through his hair, nails raking his scalp. Farid shook her touch away. He didn't want gentleness. He wanted a hard, pounding distraction to mute his pain.

Then her grip tightened. "I understand you've been through something really painful, Farid. I won't take advantage of you in this moment and have sex with you but I can hold you."

With that, she curled onto her side and tugged him in close. Her arms came around him and Farid stiffened. If she wasn't going to help ease his pain, he didn't want her here. He started to tell her that but found himself laying his head on her chest. A sob lodged in his throat but he pushed it back.

Sora stroked a hand up and down her back and Farid gazed into nothing while inside he allowed himself this moment to mourn.

Chapter 10

Sora eased from the bed quietly, hoping to leave without waking the slumbering man in the bed. She tiptoed toward his bedroom door only to be brought up short.

"Where are you going?"

She glanced back over her shoulder. Farid lay on his back, one arm thrown over his eyes, the other resting across his chest. His long hair tangled on the pillow beneath him. "I'm leaving."

Technically, she was still on shift but her tickets were complete and her work never received complaints.

Heaving upright on a groan, Farid swung his legs to the side and pressed the palms of his hands into his eyes. "Give me a moment. I'll walk you out."

While he sat hunched over on the edge of the bed, Sora remembered how good it felt to be in his arms. She couldn't recall a time when she'd done nothing more but rest next to a man. When Farid straightened and looked up, she was confronted with sorrow filled eyes.

Her heart lurched. *Damn it.* This wasn't supposed to happen. She wasn't supposed to develop any feelings on this mission. "Farid, I don't need help walking to the door."

He shoved to his feet strode toward her. Ignoring the broad body coming her way took a lot. Especially as they'd essentially spent the night together. "I need to lock the door behind you."

Her lips quirked. "I assure you I can take care of that too."

He snorted, the corner of his mouth lifting in the first semblance of lightness since she'd told him what she'd discovered. They walked in companionable silence to his door.

Farid opened it and stood to the side. Sora swallowed back what she wanted to say. He needed time.

As she neared to pass by him, she leaned forward, placed a hand on his shoulder and kissed the curve of Farid's jaw. Her lips lingered as the masculine scent of him filled her nostrils. One last inhale and she eased away. She hated to bring the topic back up but couldn't leave without saying something. "He'll pay, Farid."

She stepped through the doorway and engaged her processors to stem the odd quake in her belly. Why was leaving him so hard?

"I'm doing it."

The husky rough murmur jerked her to a stop. Sora dropped her head forward and closed her eyes on a sigh. She knew what he meant. Her first response was to refuse. Farid wasn't in an emotional place to agree on what she and Kelix wanted.

"Did you hear me? I'm doing it," he said again.

Sora turned slowly to face him. "Farid—"

Anger blazed across his face and he held the door open wider. She shoved at his chest and pushed him back inside and slammed the door shut. "Are you crazy?!"

"Garod killed my son."

Those four words stabbed at Sora's heart. "I. *Know*."

"Let me help you find your friends and when the time comes, help me to kill him."

His gaze was dead serious and Sora couldn't find it in her to deny him. "Fine. I have to go, though. If you can, get a confirmation on the identity of the last new fighters Garod plans to reveal on the holos—see if Kaito and Xion are there."

"Kaito and Xion?" he repeated.

"Yes."

"I'll take care of it."

His agreement was too eager. Sora stared into his eyes, seeking some confirmation he really could handle this. Pain and grief stared back. She sighed heavily. This wasn't going to end well. She could feel it. Opening the door again, she resolved to go straight to her room, shower and change clothes before meeting with Kelix to update him on this new development.

In the hall, Farid grasped her elbow, spun her around and kissed her. Caught off guard, she managed to grip his shoulders to keep from stumbling. He pulled away and brushed his lips against her ear. "Two witnesses just saw us kiss. Now we have a reason for you to come back here tonight and any time we're seen spending time together."

He wanted them to pretend to be lovers? Sora gaped but Farid stepped back and shut the door in her face.

***

"It's a good plan," Kelix stated when Sora updated him two days later.

"To pretend to be lovers? It's an awful idea," she protested, pacing as much as possible in the tiny maintenance closet filled with chemical supplies.

"We have a handful of days left and he's willing to search for Kaito and Xion. Pretending to be in a relationship will derail any suspicion if Farid's seen in your company too much. Unless you have a problem with the rumors it might cause."

Kelix raised his voice on the last making it an inquiry. Sora sighed and gripped the ends of her hair to tug then groaned in frustration. "You're right. It's a solid plan."

"Are you worried he'll want to make the lie true?" Kelix asked, his brows drawing together.

Snorting, Sora dropped her hand and shook her head. "No."

Her answer must have come too slow. Kelix stilled. From his position leaning against a row of shelves, his scrutiny caused her to flush. His head tipped to the side. "You had sex with him?"

"Nooo," she dragged out. Not quite. They'd slept together in the official sense of the phrase but nothing else. "He was distraught. I'd just told him the son he's fighting for is dead."

"Sooo, you had sex to apologize for telling him or not?"

Humor glinted in his midnight gaze and she stabbed a finger at him. "He wanted to but there's nothing funny about that moment, Kelix. He was devastated. I've never wanted to kill someone more. Not even Shui."

Kelix straightened and pushed away from the wall, jostling the container behind him. He gripped Sora by the upper arms. She quelled her instinct to jerk away. "You're right. That kind of news would destroy an individual but you can't deviate from the plan. We have to be careful how we play this, Sora. Those running the *Gladyx* need to be taken down but we can only do that if we watch every step we make and get all of them. Not just Garod."

She understood that. Except she kept seeing the pain barely leashed on Farid's face when she left him. "I understand."

Kelix stared a moment longer as if searching for the truth in her gaze then nodded and released her. He swiped a hand down his face. "In other matters, Cyllus received an encoded message from Reo."

That was a shock and good news. As an initial member of their group when they escaped the prison transport, Reo had vanished as soon as he heard about two women his pod brethren had saved before their untimely deaths. "What! Where is he?"

"He didn't say. Only that he believes he has the location of the women."

Sora wondered if finding the women would bring him peace. Losing a member from your pod left harsh scars on the psyche of a cyborg. Reo didn't just lose one person connected to him, he'd lost all three. He'd been withdrawn and spiraling ever since.

While Sora didn't know where her other pod mates were aside from Thalen, she did know they were out there somewhere and more importantly, alive. Her neural net processor gave off a steady hum, signaling their presence though the distance meant they couldn't mentally connect with each other. If they had died, she would have sensed a blank void just as Reo had.

"I wish he'd talked to us before leaving. We could have helped."

Kelix grunted in agreement. "Tagan is working hard trying to track him. Sooner or later we'll have his location."

And she could kick his ass for the disappearing act.

Kelix tugged at the hem of his jacket and smoothed his hand down the front. "I need to go. I have a meeting with a group of buyers for dinner. This might be the break I've been looking for to get in with the darker elements behind the scenes."

"Stay safe."

He clasped her hand. "Same."

Once he was gone, Sora exhaled heavily. She'd do everything in her power to get justice for Farid.

Chapter 11

Farid forced himself to wake bright and early. Today was the day he went to see the other fighters. His steps dragged as he made his way to the lower level behind the fight arena. Those, like him, who'd been with the *Gladyx* for a while and had established that they wouldn't try to escape were given rooms on the main floors and allowed to move around unencumbered.

Due to the nature of his arrangement, Farid had never spent time in this area so it was a shock to enter this section. Two guards stationed at the entrance recognized him instantly and moved aside with slight nods in his direction. He tipped his head at them and continued on toward the center aisle, separating rows of dorm styled rooms.

Doors weren't necessary for these fighters as they would be killed the moment they attempted to leave this area.

At the first opening, he peered inside at a contender stretched on a simple cot, arms folded behind his head. They'd fought twice in the past with Farid winning both matches. They hadn't been death bouts.

He moved from one opening to another until he reached the end of the aisle. Here were the newer fighters. And cages. Farid wasn't stupid. He'd heard but never seen with his own eyes. Cages lined against one another held individuals considered highly dangerous. They didn't want to be here, weren't committed by blackmail and would try to escape at the first opportunity.

More than likely, Farid's final two fights would be against someone in this area.

"Look who's around early. Taking a look at the competition, huh?"

Farid tensed and slowly turned to face Mizra, another fighter, who believed himself better than the rest. They hadn't been pit against each other because Garod didn't want to risk his two best investments.

He turned away from Mizra. His words meant little to Farid. There was no pleasure in what he did in the arena. And with Sora's revelation, there wasn't even a point to it now.

"Farid?"

Glancing over at him in irritation, Farid arched a brow. "What do you want, Mizra?"

"When I saw you coming this way, I thought wouldn't it be great if we judged the competition together?"

Moving forward on a huff, Farid didn't answer. He and Mizra weren't friends and had never pretended such. In fact, the only pretense Farid had ever taken part of was the one he'd proposed to Sora. Lovers. There hadn't been a consistent lover in his bed since he signed his contract for the *Gladyx*.

Women came and went. Many of the female visitors to the fights and sometimes spouses and mates to buyers offered themselves freely to Farid. He could have a steady stream in his bed if he chose. But he hadn't. Other than an occasional bed mate to relieve tension, Farid stayed to himself to avoid another situation like Ashme.

Now, he'd committed himself to Sora. Or more apt, her cause. All morning, he'd been unable to completely dismiss their evening together. There had been no sex but the intimacy of the moment couldn't be denied. It was the height of irony that he'd once dreamed of meeting a partner, starting a family and spending his remaining years making Turin happy. None of that was necessary anymore.

"What do you think of the Nagani?" Mizra asked, breaking into Farid's thoughts.

Thudded steps confirmed the other fighter stayed on his heels.

"What's to think?" Farid stopped in front of the cage housing the serpentine male. Bindor, according to the introduction, rested on his purple coiled tail and stared off into the distance.

The Nagani were peaceful and eschewed violence unless necessary. Having one here purely to fight in games to amuse the audience spoke to Garod and the others lack of care outside their greed.

Mizra stared at Bindor and threw his hands toward the cage. "Look at him. No one's ever fought one before. If you can make one mad enough, it will be quite the show for the crowd."

Farid curled his lip in disgust and ignored Mizra to go to the next cage and the Cepphi inside. At their approach, he snarled and slammed a suction covered tentacle against the bars of the cage. Mizra jumped then laughed self consciously.

Moving along, Farid concentrated on the last few cages. One held the Doorian with the single eye. Bommba glared as he continued using the top bar of his cage to do chin ups steadily, but it was the last two that brought Farid's steps to a halt. The cages were side by side and held a single occupant each—two males with dark hair and wearing only battered pants.

Both glanced up and sneered, revealing a facial brand Farid immediately recognized. The letters CR were etched in a dark stain on their cheeks. According to Sora, knowledge of these cyborgs' whereabouts put them in grave danger.

Yet Garod, Urson, and Parson had made no effort to hide the vivid brand and planned on having them fight for all to see. Not to mention the announcement vid scheduled for later which would more than likely feature these two prominently.

After Sora's casual show of strength with his door, Farid believed these two would be a surprise to any opponent. He wouldn't underestimate what these men were capable of.

"Huh. They look frail. Not much of a challenge," Mizra muttered beside him.

If Mizra thought that, he was blind. While the men didn't move, the look in their eyes promised retribution at the very first chance.

Feigning disinterest, Farid turned away. "I need to rest."

"Do you have a fight tonight I don't know about," Mizra asked with a smug grin.

It wasn't like others weren't aware of Farid's contract. Those who'd been on the *Gladyx* long enough also knew he had a son. Tok Su was one of them and Mizra was the other.

Neither had ever mentioned Turin before. Thinking of his son brought back Farid's rage and his gaze narrowed on Mizra as he grabbed his shirt and slammed him against the bars of the cage on the left, holding one of the cyborgs.

Mizra batted at his arms but Farid locked his fingers and leaned in close to snarl, "Do you think something's funny?"

"Wh-what's wrong with you?!" Mizra choked out, struggling in his hold.

Using his grip, Farid lifted Mizra and tossed him to the side. He slid across the floor and immediately sprung to his feet in a crouch. Farid sneered and turned his back on him. Guards raced over but he ignored them and made his way toward the exit.

Mizra ranted, trying to explain Farid had attacked him. The guards wouldn't touch Farid. They knew better.

***

"They're here," Farid announced when Sora opened her door.

Eyes bleary from staying up late to create small wiring issues in the *Gladyx*'s mainframe to slow the ship from reaching Hanass, she stared blankly. "Huh?"

"Your friends. I found them here."

Laughter from two guests as they walked down the hall interrupted them. The women's gazes paused on Farid's broad figure standing in her doorway. Appreciation glimmered in their eyes as their pace slowed. It was obvious they recognized him. Their hungry looks devoured him and left no secret to the thoughts in their minds.

Unexpected jealousy unfurled in Sora's belly. She shot a glare at them. Smiling, Farid caressed Sora's hair and leaned over to kiss her. Thoughts of how she could teach the women not to look at things that didn't belong to them faded. Her mouth softened beneath the weight of Farid's and she absorbed the wild berry taste of his lips.

Passion and desire exploded, causing her to wrap her hands around his neck and clench tight. His groan was muffled by her tongue dipping and swirling in his mouth. She wasn't so far gone she didn't notice him walking her backward into her room and kicking the door shut.

As soon as it closed, he ended the kiss. Sora blinked. Farid jammed a hand through his hair then folded his arms over his chest. "Lovers."

The single word was explanation enough. "Right."

He'd kissed her to fool anyone around. Then the rest of what he'd said earlier sank in. Her senses came alive and excitement had her pressing down on her bare feet to tame the urge to punch her fist in the air. "Kaito and Xion are here?"

"Yes. In the caged section with dangerous new fighters. Both wearing a brand similar to the one you showed me."

Sora nibbled her bottom lip. If the conglomerate chose to have them fight without hiding the rebel marks, Kirs authorities and the emperor would be here in an instant. There were only three more days before they reached the station stop. If others knew cyborgs were onboard, they might chance a takeover of the *Gladyx* or sneak in to claim the reward from Shui.

"Is there anyway you can get me down to see them?" she asked.

Farid was already shaking his head in the negative. "You've been down there once and didn't caught. To go again would put you at risk."

"Fuck!" Sora drove her fingers through her hair and turned away from him. "I have to do something."

"Are you open to a suggestion?"

The quiet question sent Sora spinning back around to face him. Farid's arms dropped to his side and he closed the distance she'd created between them. His hazel eyes creased at the corners and Sora resisted the urge to lean into him. "What are you thinking?"

Farid tucked a loose strand of hair behind her ear. "Lay low. Take your time and plan with whoever is here working with you. Don't do anything rash to draw attention to yourself."

His idea held merit. The ease with which he made the suggestion also implied he'd calmed a little from the raging anger of the night when he'd discovered the truth about Turin.

Sora exhaled softly and admitted. "I hear what you're saying but I don't have much time. Knowing they're here has increased the urgency. We have to get off this ship before it arrives at Hanass."

"So we have a few days."

She didn't comment on his *we*. Sora wouldn't refuse his help. This was exactly what they'd wanted when the goal was to get a fighter on their side. She met his stare evenly. "A few days to get Kaito and Xion free and then bring down the conglomerate."

Farid went to move away from her but suddenly turned back. He caught her arm and tugged. Caught off guard, Sora stumbled forward. He dipped his head down and kissed her. Sora gasped and he took advantage of her open mouth.

His lips parted and his hands gripped her hips as he groaned. His tongue tangled with hers in rough, urgent strokes, kissing her with a hint of desperation. Sora met his ferocity with an anger all her own.

Anger at Garod, anger at all those on the *Gladyx* participating in the oppression of the fighters here against their will. And beneath all that fury, a shift occurred. Desire overruled the anger. Sora rocked against Farid's hard frame, the swell of his erection hardening along her belly.

Sliding her hands into the loose black hair falling about their faces, she strained to get closer. Farid nipped at her mouth, his hands running feverishly up and down her back.

Sora couldn't get enough. When he eased his leg between her thighs, his knee notched at her crotch. Tiny zings shot up her spine from the contact and her head fell back on a gasp.

"Are you opposed to sex now?" he whispered.

A smile broke across her face. Sora's answer was to reach down and caress the length of him through his pants. "Here or in my bed?"

***

An unexpected wave of relief washed over Farid. She hadn't refused him. Her acceptance acted as a tiny patch on the huge gaping hole where his heart used to be.

"Your bed." Not that it mattered to Farid. He could have thrown her to the floor right here and dealt with the desire blazing through him but a modicum of decency reared its head.

"Fine with me." Gaze soft, she raised both of her hands and ran them through his hair.

Grabbing her wrist, he growled. "Show me."

She led him to her bedroom and he followed with a level of trust he hadn't given anyone in years. But Sora deserved it. She'd held him, accepted his pain and given him a small slice of peace in return.

In her room, he headed straight for the bed and with a slight shove to the chest, pushed Sora backward onto it. She sat up on her elbows and pulled the tab of her jumper down to her waist, revealing a black fitted tank top beneath.

Next the tank went up and over her head to land at the bottom of his bed. Round breasts with large areoles and stubby nipples sat high on her chest. Farid dove on the bed and cupped one in each hand. He lowered his head and sucked a spongy bud into his mouth.

Sora moaned and fell back but her fingers latched onto his hair, tugging the thick strands. Farid moved to the opposite side and laved the fullness of her other breast before drawing the tight bud in his mouth. She arched up under him and he used his weight to press her back down on the bed.

Already hard, his cock throbbed. Farid reached down with one hand to adjust and Sora took the opportunity to slide from under him. He eyed her in confusion but she tossed him a saucy smile and hooked her fingers in the bottom half of the maintenance jumper and shove it down.

"This works better if we're both naked."

Her words spurred him on and Farid ripped his shirt off, uncaring of the rough treatment to his clothes. His pants received the same lack of consideration and he kicked them off.

Standing beside his bed, grief swelled like a tide coming through and he needed to purge his mind of every thought or he'd go insane. When he returned to the bed, he didn't take time to admire Sora's body, too desperate to give in to the urge to taste every inch of her exposed skin.

Later, he'd do that later.

Lowering himself over her, he gripped his cock in hand and settled between her thighs. He nudged her entrance and she parted her legs wide, hands going to his shoulders. "I can take it."

Farid took her at her word and surged forward. Her body eased for him and he sank deep. Wet heat surrounded him as her channel pulsed and rippled along the length of his cock.

Bracing his hands at the sides of her head, he pushed up and rocked back. Sora's long legs rose and hooked around his hips. Her head tipped back, baring the slim line of her throat. Farid plunged forward. Again. And again.

Blinding pleasure spread over his mind and heart. Sensations rolled over his body and arousal licked up his cock and settled in his gut.

The cadence of Sora's breathing changed, became ragged as she panted and clutched him close. He closed his eyes and focused on giving her what she'd unselfishly given him. His hips pounded at her and his heart raced. The soft clasp of her internal muscles worked his cock, shoving him closer and closer to orgasm.

His back hunched and he groaned as his sac tightened against him. He hooked a hand under Sora's right knee and lifted it higher as he leaned forward. A hoarse grunt tore from his throat and his seed shot from his cock in a stream. As soon as he emptied the last drop, Farid pulled out and slid down to place his mouth on Sora's wet entrance.

He fluttered his tongue fast and hard between her slit and she cried out, thighs clamping about his head. He worked two fingers in her hole, causing her body to twist and dance in her pleasure.

Raising his gaze only, he watched. Every moan and gasp rewarded his efforts. Moments later, she arched up on a sharp cry and her body bucked violently. He flattened his forearm over her midsection to keep her in place while her orgasm sent shudders coursing through her lean, muscular frame.

When she stilled and slumped to the bed on a weak gasp, he moved back up over her and growled, "Again."

He gripped her hip and entered her on one fierce stroke and sought oblivion between her legs.

Chapter 12

The next day flew by. On a cloud of bliss, Sora took her break and went back to her room. She was relaxed after her night with Farid and made the mistake of turning on the vid screen. What she saw left her stunned and she couldn't look away.

The *Gladyx* had just showed Kaito and Xion sitting inside cages, their faces on full display—along with their cyborg rebellion brand.

"What has he done?" she whispered as fear lashed at her.

The few days she and Farid had gambled on no longer existed. It was only a matter of time before someone informed Shui or a desperate mercenary showed in an attempt to claim the reward by taking a cyborg back to Kirs.

In the background of the promo, Garod's voice droned on about the two new opponents, the upcoming matches and when betting would open.

Sora gave her attention to the time slots that popped up over the frozen images of Kaito and Xion. The first fights would occur this afternoon, a total of four on the schedule. Kaito's match would be one of them, pitting him against Zozo, the crying giant she'd seen in the cages.

No good could come of that. With his enhanced strength and military training, Kaito would decimate Zozo. The knock at her door pulled Sora's attention away from the vid. Thinking it was Kelix in a rage, she hurried to answer and didn't bother scanning first.

"We can work this out," she said as she swung the door open.

"Work out what?" Farid asked as he came in.

Sora closed the door automatically, eyeing his brawny form from head to toe. He wore a black shirt that hugged his large frame and black pants with matching boots. The dark clothing drew attention to the mottled color of his skin.

Coming to a stop in her living room, he turned and faced Sora. "You mentioned working something out. What does that mean?"

She shook her head. No way was she getting into how she thought he was Kelix. "Nothing. What brings you here?"

"I saw the vid and wanted to check on you."

Sora blew out a breath and moved to the kitchen nook to pour a glass of water. "I know. They just ran the promo on the vid screen of the *dangerous* new additions."

Farid followed her and leaned his forearms on the small counter ledge. "That means everyone will know they're here before the day is out."

A bitter snort escaped. "Everyone will know sooner because one of them, Kaito, already has a fight lined up."

Farid froze. Sora lowered her cup from her mouth to see what had changed. She met his stare and caught a glimpse of anguish before he masked his expression and shifted his gaze to the side. Knowledge slammed into her and Sora could have kicked herself.

The fight assigned to Kaito must have been originally scheduled for Farid. There was no horror dark enough to inflict on Garod for his actions. The level of evil in what he and the conglomerate were doing to Farid went beyond words.

"I'm sorry, Farid."

He brushed her off with a muttered sound and pushed upright. "I came to tell you about the announcement but since you're aware, I'll leave."

"No, no, no." Setting her cup down, she moved closer to him and touched his hand. A spark popped from her fingertips and he twitched. Sora flushed. She hadn't made a mistake like that since she'd first received her cybernetics. "This has got be awful for you but I need to get to Kaito. I know you said it would draw attention to us, but I need to speak to him and let him know we're here to get him out. It can't wait any longer. Can you help me with that?"

His muscles tensed then eased. "I said I'd help in anyway, Sora. I haven't changed my mind."

"Okay." He wasn't behaving the way she'd expected after they'd had sex. Which was fine. She dropped her hand and ignored the tingles left behind from touching his bare skin. "Do you think it would be a problem to go before the fight?"

Sora couldn't think of a way to prevent the fight but at least Kaito would know Kelix was here and that his rescue was imminent. It might give him the motivation and drive he needed to hang on. She had no idea of his mental state or that of Xion's.

Farid ran a forefinger under his bottom lip as he thought. "I've already gone down and it might put Garod and the others on alert if I go back."

Fuck. He was right. But. "What if I pretend to be excited? Maybe begged you to take me there."

"Use the lover angle?"

Sora fought back a shiver at the telling gleam in his eyes. They were both remembering that night. "Yes."

The corner of his lips curved up and the change in his face knocked the breath from her lungs. Damn dimples. "That could work. It's something that comes up often enough for some. When do you want to go?"

"Now?" The sooner, the better. Getting the two cyborgs out was the reason she was here. She added kicking Garod's ass to her to do list.

"Too soon." Farid held up a hand stopping the next words out of her mouth. "We can walk around though, get anyone watching used to our presence. It will cause less attention when we do go down. Call it a tour."

While she wanted to race off to the fighter area, it wouldn't be smart to reveal their hand before she and Kelix were ready. Plus, she needed to make sure Kelix remained calm because she was certain he'd caught the vid screen reveal just like she had. "Fine."

Chapter 13

Farid didn't know what compelled him to offer Sora a tour. His plan had been to tell her about her friends and return to his room. He needed to figure out how to get off the *Gladyx* if the conglomerate refused to give him any more fights.

Then there was the implanted explosive in his wrist. He'd need a specialist to remove that. It would please Garod to no end to detonate it the moment Farid stepped off the cruiser. Farid wouldn't give him the pleasure. He'd find a way to get off this ship with his life intact and take Garod and the conglomerate down in the process.

"What's down here?" Sora asked from the left of him.

She'd been silent so far during the walk. Farid had decided to show her the restricted areas limited for fighter access only. Even as a maintenance tech, she would have needed special permission to be on this side of the cruiser.

"Weight rooms, kitchens, isolation chambers," he rattled off all the places he'd been and knew by heart.

Her head tipped up and she cast a glance at him. "Isolation chambers?"

Up ahead, two fighters came around the corner. Farid wrapped an arm around Sora's shoulders, ignoring the way she stiffened. The fighters nodded at Farid, eyed Sora then continued on without slowing their pace.

Warmth emanated along his side where their bodies brushed against one another with each step. Visions of her parted lips and flush body mid-orgasm bombarded his mind. Farid cleared his throat. "Isolation chambers are for when a fighter wants to be alone to align his mind, body and spirit. The doors seal for the set time programmed in and you can't get out until it expires."

The sound she made was one of derision. "Not my idea of fun."

An unexpected spurt of amusement hit Farid. "It's not supposed to be fun. It's to relax you before or after a fight."

She snorted and arched her brows. "Have you ever done it?"

"Yes. There's not much I haven't done in my ten years here." He was sure she probably expected him to say no.

"Why would anyone want to do that?"

Farid slowed their steps near the kitchen. This was the one place he frequented often and didn't cause him stress. He shouldered the door open, welcoming the smell of roasting vegetables, the clink of dishware and the mutters of Greta, the head cook.

With her back to the door, Greta yelled, "Who's in here? No visitors allowed!"

"It's me," Farid called, continuing to lead Sora to the side of a counter filled with covered dishes and the stool that hadn't moved in the five years since he'd started visiting.

Greta spun around with a welcome smile on her blue face. The Zudan's multiple arms waved in the air, several holding utensils and spices. "Farid! Help yourself. I always keep stuff prepared for you just in case."

Guiding Sora to sit on the stool, Farid pulled several bowls toward the space in front of her. "Thank you, Greta."

"Mmhmm." Ignoring Sora, she turned back around to the various pots cooking on the heating elements lined across the kitchen mount station.

"What's all of this?" Sora asked, eyeing the dishes of steaming food.

Farid leaned behind her, arms bracketed her slim form and pointed to the bowls. "After my fights, I'm usually drained. Gurzals need to eat a lot after a large expenditure of energy. Because my matches tend to be the last on the schedule, nothing's available to eat that late. Greta keeps her kitchen open for me."

Sora leaned over a bowl of steaming noodles. "Can't you eat in your room? Use the food processor."

Heat filled his cheeks and his mouth hovered over the delicate curve of her ear. "Gurzals are vegetable eaters. The processors in our room mainly serve meat. Too much of that and we sicken. Greta prepares what I need in large quantities."

Greta hummed behind him and Farid bit back a grin. He moved to the side of Sora and grabbed a bowl of leafy greens. He picked up a wrapped utensil and uncovered it to shovel a mouthful in. Sora tentatively tasted the noodles. Her expression brightened and they ate until Farid couldn't take another bite.

Only two of the six containers remained. Sora had consumed her fair share, impressing him. She spun on her stool, facing him. One hand came to rest on his hip and the other leaned on the counter. Her touch ignited tiny fires at the point of contact through his clothing.

"That was pretty good. I can see why you'd come here," she said.

Farid shrugged, not wanting her to know how much her touch affected him. Greta humphed behind them.

"Come on. Let's go." He cupped her elbow and helped Sora to her feet. She followed behind him, waving at Greta who flicked one of her arms in their direction and kept cooking with the others as they left.

Farid led her down a narrow hall, off the main course. There was less traffic due to the time of day and because the only thing in this area were the isolation chambers.

He stopped in front of the door to one of them. It had been a while since he'd used one. At first the quiet and calming solitude had helped him to deal with the fights and deaths. Then they'd become a place to over think everything that happened in the arena which *wasn't* good for him.

Sora glanced around, no sign of fear. "Where are we?"

"Isolation chambers are on this side." He lowered his voice. "It's safer to talk."

***

"You asked me an important question once and I'm ready to answer," Farid continued. "You pretty much have it figured out. No one leaves because of the threats and no one's ever caught because this cruiser stays on the move. Authorities don't care enough to investigate because Garod, Urson and Parson don't take anyone considered important."

"Damn them!" Sora spun away from the row of doors with no windows to face him. Kaito and Xion *were* important. Just not to anyone around here. They were decorated military soldiers who deserved better than to be forced into this brutal game.

"Shhh!"

Moving around her, Farid unlatched the heavy framed door, set the timer on the box to the right of the jamb and placed his hand on her lower back, shoving her forward. Sora stumbled inside. The locking mechanism clicked in place with a solid thud.

There was a single woven mat on the floor. Steam shot from the vents above and the lights turned off. "What the?!"

Farid kept his hand on her and guided her to where he'd last seen the mat. His boot kicked the cloth and he tugged Sora down. "Anyone can hear in the hall. We can talk freely in here. The conglomerate isn't interested in listening to fighters meditate."

He went down to his knees next to her and breathed deeply of the thick air being pumped in. His voice was hushed when he spoke. "The cyborgs you're looking for are in separate cages next to each other. As you saw in the vid-screen promo, the brand on their faces was fully on display. The *Gladyx* doesn't care if your emperor sees it."

It was hard to focus on what he said now that they were in the enclosed space. Sora's heart rate sped up and her pulse thumped madly. Having ocular implants meant her vision wasn't impaired from the darkness but that didn't still the rising panic triggered by being in an enclosed space.

The more she inhaled, the more the manufactured air attempted to relax her. Viewing the change as a chemical attack, the nanobots in her body rapidly filtered the effects in defense. She clenched her hands in her lap and tried to calm her nerves by focusing on what she could see, hear and control.

Like right now, she could hear the slow and steady breaths Farid took. He sat back on his knees, hands resting on his thighs, palm sides up. She admired the stillness he held himself with while fear and paranoia batted at her senses.

"Is it a drug?" Sora whispered from beside him in reference to the effect of whatever additive mixed with the steam in here.

Farid inhaled and seemed to relax even more. "No. Natural oils and herbs. The medical facility developed it for a fighter who struggled with his mental acuity before his matches. The plants they use are from his world and were discovered to have a calming affect on other beings."

Which implied a chemical of some sort released from the plant. That explained why her nanobots were fighting. Her brain continued to send an urgent alert to her body and it kept responding. She worked hard to stop the effect but Sora couldn't shake the memory of the events on the prison transport—being locked in a cell with cyborgs she didn't know or trust.

Farid brushed a hand over her tense leg. "If you want to save your friends, you have to be careful. You can't charge in without a plan, a thorough one, or the conglomerate will destroy all of you."

It was hard to focus on anything he said. Panting, Sora drove her hands through her hair then took a deep breath and let it out. Between the herbs and her processors, her emotions fluctuated in disarray. "Once we get Kaito and Xion out, we plan to steal an emergency shuttle and leave."

He snorted in disbelief beside her. "The conglomerate will never let you steal a ship and leave. There's security all over."

Heat rose around her collar and sweat trickled down her forehead. Her breathing sped up again, forcing her systems into overdrive but she focused enough to answer Farid. "You have no idea of what we're capable of. A single cyborg should never be underestimated. A team of cyborgs is even more deadly."

"Dead is dead, Sora." The tone of his voice changed, softened. "I've got enough guilt on my plate."

Sympathy tugged at her heart but before she could touch on it, a loud hiss came from above. Sora jerked. More steam rained down in a burst. She flinched, the sound throwing her violently back into the past.

'Treason. Sentence to serve time on Tyurma.'

The emperor's words rang like a death knell in her head. Energy cuffs. Being separated from her pod and forced into a cell onboard a transport ship.

Sora was locked inside with a group of cyborgs she barely knew and unable to contact the other three members of her pod. An urgent message blasted on the open mainframe. The emperor plotted to kill them. The transport ships they were on were going to blow.

Cyllus, Reo, Tagan and Kelix argued amongst themselves on what to do. Heart in her throat, she studied the composition of the energy shield holding them in here. As much as she hated to think of it, her conversion from a dedicated soldier to one of the Cyborg Elite Military had come with a few side effects. One of them was her strange ability to manipulate energy.

It was something Sora had only shared with her own pod grouping. She glared at the walls of the cell and a surge of anger blasted from her gut. She refused to die like this.

Sora pushed off from the wall she'd been leaning on to where Cyllus stood by their only exit. She vaguely knew of the other cyborg. His strong reputation for being good at his missions and a fearless leader preceded him. She wasn't at the point where she trusted any of them enough to share her secret but in this instance, there was no choice.

'There are no tumblers or electronic locks for us to bypass,' Cyllus told her as she drew near.

Sora shot an annoyed glare in his direction. 'I know that!'

The others gathered close. Tagan's gravelly voice rumbled, 'Getting off the transport won't be an issue if we can't get out of our cell.'

They could steal or hack anything with their cybernetics if a system was powered and online. This would require more. Sora held her hand up to the barrier. The energy shield was a different construct but her blood pulsed and flickers came to life beneath her skin.

'What's she doing?' Cyllus asked.

Ignoring the voices to concentrate on the power flowing from her fingertips, Sora braced her weight. The rhythmic timing was the key. She just had to figure out the frequency of the currents in the shield and disrupt the pattern.

The moment she increased the power from within, lightning lit her insides like a flaming sword. This was bigger than anything she'd tried before. So much energy flowing to and from her. A grimace twisted her mouth as it took everything in Sora not to move back and away from the pain.

Tension held her shoulders rigid and dots of moisture glistened on her forehead. Then it happened. A weakness in the field, causing the barrier to dim. Once. Twice.

Beside her, Cyllus stiffened. His fingers curled at his sides in clenched fists. Hope blazed from his gaze, encouraging Sora to hold on even as agony tore up her arm.

A thousand needles jabbed and sliced at the skin of her forearm. Her arm shook and her teeth chattered. Then with a light buzz, the shielded door dropped. There one moment, then gone. The cessation of that many currents coursing through her body jolted.

'Fuuuck!' Sora cried out. She stumbled back and dropped her arm to her side.

The energy she'd absorbed partially settled in her belly like a fiery ball. She gasped in wrenching gulps of air then clasped her arms about her midsection with a sharp yelp. Her back shuddered with the force of trying to get herself under control. She muffled her heavy breathing by clamping her lips tight and sensed them all tensing.

Was she malfunctioning? What if she'd damaged herself permanently in her efforts to free them?

Seconds later, Sora forced herself upright with a garbled growl. Her gray eyes sparked with fire as she glanced around the quiet forms studying her.

"Sora!" Farid yelled her name and shook her.

She snapped out of the vivid memory. His stark features were alight with fear. "What?"

Her voice was a husky, hoarse rasp. Trembles shook her frame and chill bumps peppered her all over. Farid ran his hands up and down her arms. "You're freezing."

He slid around behind her, legs bracketing her own as his arms wrapped firmly around her middle to tug her back against his chest.

The unexpected embrace distilled the last of the nightmare clinging to her skin. Farid lowered his head and rested his jaw on the junction between her shoulder and neck. "Hang on. It won't be much longer now. The door will open soon."

Gazing around in confusion, Sora settled her racing heartbeat. The fear of earlier no longer hammered at her.

"I have you," Farid reassured in a whisper near her ear.

Sora attempted to turn to see his face but his arms were like a vise around her waist. The dark interior pinged at her senses again. She latched onto his wrists with clinging fingers.

Drawing in deep breaths, Sora closed her eyes and settled her weight back against him. Farid's touch soothed as it aroused. She let these new feelings overcome the ones of terror. It took effort but she banished the memory from the prison transport to the back of her mind where it belonged. What had happened to them was in the past and nothing could change that.

Farid's thighs lay like sentinels alongside her own but twice as thick. His arms bulged with muscle yet held her with a gentleness she wouldn't have attributed to the same fighter who killed with seeming disinterest in the arena.

She stroked his forearms in an absentminded touch, letting his presence ground her in the here and now. Behind her, Farid shifted slightly in reaction to her caresses. Firm lips pressed to the open collar of her maintenance jumper.

Chapter 14

Worry had taken hold of Farid when Sora suddenly stilled beside him. Her silence scared him and she hadn't responded to his tap on the shoulder or him calling her name. Her muffled cry pierced his heart in a space previously reserved only for Turin. Instinct had him reaching to shake her from whatever trance she'd fallen into.

With her settled between the apex of his legs, nestled close against him, he absorbed the weight of her warm body. Holding a woman was a rarity. Before or after sex. Having Sora trust him by not fighting his embrace spoke volumes. It was easy to discern she wasn't one to give her trust easily.

Neither was Farid.

Her trembling eased and he continued to keep her pressed close to his chest. Whatever memory had suddenly assaulted her had left its mark. Farid hadn't expected to see such fractures in a woman who'd exemplified strength in their short acquaintance. He nuzzled the side of her throat, unable to resist giving her a reminder that she wasn't alone.

The soft sigh she released encouraged him. Farid pressed his lips to the sliver of skin revealed by the loose collar of her uniform. Her soft skin worked as a balm to his own senses. She lightly trailed her nails across the top of his wrists and he groaned. Easing closer, Farid slowly turned her around, giving her ample time to break away if she chose.

When he had her facing him, Sora straddled his lap and settled her groin directly over his cock. Another groan broke free. Her hands delved straight into his hair and she arched back pressing their lower halves together intimately.

Forgetting his intention had been to ease whatever tormented her memories, Farid cupped the back of her head in the palm of his hand and brought her in close. His mouth crushed onto her in a kiss driven by need, desire and remnants of sadness.

Focusing on the physical sensations she created in him was better than letting his mind wander to the jagged holes in his chest formed by the loss of Turin.

She moaned and rocked against him with frantic jerks. Farid fumbled around and moved his hands between their heaving chests. He managed to lower the tab on Sora's jumpsuit halfway down to free her bound breasts. Shoving the material up, he stared in awe at the bouncing globes.

Sora grinned and pushed the hair back from his forehead. "Don't just stare."

A grin tickled the corners of his mouth. Farid leaned forward and tugged her up enough to nuzzle then suck the taut pink bud of her nipple. Sora cried out. This time in pleasure, not fear. Farid inhaled her sweet aroma, licking and laving his way to the left and the exposed curve of her other full breast.

"Yes," Sora hissed, grounding her hips down on him.

Farid caught her at the hips and jerked her back to devour her mouth. Her lips parted in shock and his tongue slid through. The taste of her exploded on the tip of his tongue. He stroked the inner recesses of her mouth, hungry for every bit of Sora.

Sweet. She was sweeter than the berries he ate for breakfast.

"BZZZ!"

A loud click followed the buzzing sound. They broke apart on a pant. Farid surged to his feet, still holding Sora in his arms. She pushed away from his grasp on a shuddering breath.

"The lock," he muttered.

The door to the isolation chamber had released and they were free to leave.

Sora blew out a breath. "Right."

Side by side, they walked toward the door. Farid caught her hand before she opened it. "Sora, be careful. I don't trust the conglomerate. They'll do anything they have to in order to keep things the way they are."

Her fingers entwined with his and she opened the door with her free hand. In the bright light of the hall, Farid squinted. Sora leaned up to kiss his cheek and whispered, "I know."

Then she let his hand go and wiggled her fingers in his direction as she started walking away backward. "Don't forget to come get me later before the fights. After, we can go to the arena together."

Farid stiffened. He didn't usually go to the matches if he wasn't scheduled. His plan had been to take her to see the fighters and speak to the two cyborgs. Knowing Sora would be at the fights, alone, and planning something risky to see her cyborg friends free changed his mind. He'd be there. If only to make sure no one hurt her.

The conglomerate had taken enough from him.

***

As she hurried away, Sora rubbed her fingers briskly over her tender lips. What was wrong with her? She'd gone from a terrifying flashback to practically humping Farid in the span of minutes. Sexual frenzy wasn't something she associated with herself but what else could she use to describe this reaction she kept having to the big fighter.

The two of them got together and boom, explosives—only the good kind and not the deadly ones.

Sora kept her head down and using her innate sense of direction, made her way back to the unrestricted side of the ship. No one had stopped her or looked at her twice so she could only assume her presence with Farid had been noted. She arrived in her room and went straight for the loose floorboard to bring out the comm.

Several alerts from Kelix were marked urgent. Swiping a hand across her forehead, she entered his comm code and paced. He answered with a gruff, "Can't talk much now. One of the buyers wants to tell me something important he thinks I need to know."

"The conglomerate ran a promo of their new fighters and I saw Kaito and Xion. Kaito is scheduled today to fight," she said quickly.

Kelix cursed. "It's why I was trying to reach you. This is bigger than we thought. Apparently, there's something in the works. Something big to impress the audience. No one knows any more details than that."

Sora bit her inner cheek. She didn't like that. Not at all. "Are we sticking to the plan?"

"Yes. Just moving our time table up."

Farid's warning in mind, she asked, "When?"

"Tonight, after the fights when everyone is celebrating," he said.

This was way faster than their original plan. Cyllus and Tagan weren't expecting Kelix and Sora to act for another three days. Moving the timeline up this drastically meant a fast and hard attack followed by rapid rescue. "Are we sure that's a good idea?"

"It's the only way. My sensors are on high alert. None of this feels right."

Now that he mentioned it. Her skin itched too. Sora had put it on the unexpected connection and attraction to Farid. But what if it were more? To ignore a potential fuck up was stupid. "Will you notify Cyllus and Tagan?"

"Yes."

Firming her lips, she said, "Tonight it is."

"I gotta go. Stay safe."

Kelix disconnected the call and Sora hoped they weren't making a big mistake. After her shift, she'd stop by and see Kellina and Kaylen one more time before meeting up with Farid to go to Kaito and Xion.

With that in mind, Sora stored her comm in the hiding space, deleting the last comm log with Kelix. She stood and checked her room to make sure nothing looked out of the ordinary. Her room hadn't been searched in a while. Maybe the powers that be finally believed she was who she said she was. If so, it could only work in Sora's favor.

Steps casual, she walked through the halls, calling out greetings and nodding at those who spoke. Being part of the maintenance team usually gave her the cloak of acceptability.

Everyone on the ship ignored the tech and repair individuals for the most part unless they needed something.

But Sora's *wanted* to be seen. She needed her location noted to give her credibility when she showed with Farid to *ooh* and *ahh* over the new fighters.

Goal in mind, Sora checked the mini tablet she carried as part of her job and completed each repair issue one after the other. Hours later and last assignment finished, she headed for the maintenance department.

Two taps on the door of the office and a feminine voice from inside called out, "Enter!"

Sora grinned at Kellina working hard on a holo screen illuminated in front of her and Kaylen asleep with his firm jaw propped on his fist. It wasn't the first time she'd caught one of them catching a quick nap. Simin worked them harder than any of the other call center techs but the twins never complained.

"I was just stopping in to say I cleared my queue early," Sora offered in a hushed voice.

Kellina stopped what she was working on and glanced over her shoulder. Her eyes brightened. Nothing killed her mood and Sora envied her that fortitude. "Hey, Sora. Don't worry. He sleeps hard."

Sora came in further and propped her hip on the side of their shared desk. Disheveled hair fell over Kaylen's wide brow giving him a boyish appeal. Long lashes lay like feathers over his closed lids and a dot of drool hovered at the corner of his downturned lips.

A grin tweaked Sora's mouth. He'd hate knowing she saw that. Kaylen was quite the ladies man and at any other time she'd have followed up on his flirtations to see where it led. Kellina had expressed she was flexible in terms of a sexual partner but Kaylen stated firmly he preferred women and there would be no men acting as a third in the bedroom with them.

But Sora was here under false pretenses and it wouldn't have been fair to the young siblings to get involved.

"What can I help you with?" Kellina asked in her chipper voice.

"I'm done for the day." Sora waved her tablet in the air. "Just need you to log me out. I'm excited to get over to the arena."

"No problem. Give me a moment." Kellina turned around and tapped out a bunch of keys then closed the holo screen and opened another. When she was done, she smacked her brother on the side of his head. "You're good, Sora."

Kaylen's elbow slid out from under him, before he jerked upright. Kellina spun their chair around firmly and Sora muffled a grin at his dazed look. "Hi, Kaylen."

His gaze sharpened and he smoothed a hand over his head. "Hey there, Sora. Can I help you with anything?"

"No. Kellina took care of me while you slept."

His cheeks filled with fiery red streaks and Sora laughed again as she stood up. "Thanks both of you. I have to get going."

"Maybe I'll see you later and you'll let me take care of you next time." His eyebrows wiggled suggestively.

Sora chuckled on her way to the door. "Not sure Farid would be okay with that."

Apparently the rumors had circulated like Farid said because Kaylen blanched and groaned as she shut the door behind her.

Chapter 15

A few minutes after she'd showered and changed into a pair of black tactical pants and a short sleeve black shirt, Farid arrived. She opened the door and he grabbed her hips yanking her in close. His mouth was on hers before she could blink. Sora gave into the kiss and wrapped her arms around his neck, holding on.

Just as quickly, he released her, leaned his face to the side of hers and murmured, "Parson followed me down."

She flicked a glance over his shoulder, noting someone watching but not the conglomerate member. When the man in the hall met Sora's gaze, he scurried ahead. Two others in the hall slowed and made no effort to pretend not to stare.

Farid released her and reached down to grasp her hand. Though his hazel eyes remained dark, his voice lightened when he spoke. "I hate being away from you. Let's see the fighters before the matches start. I know how excited you get."

Sora played along with the rapid switch and smiled brightly at him. "I've been waiting all day for this since you promised."

He squeezed her fingers twice and she picked up on the signal and squeezed back. Together they took the lift to the lower levels, bypassed the entrance Sora had used the last time and went through another door marked assigned personnel only. When she looked at him askance, he tipped his head to the side and guided her forward.

Workers and fighters paused at the sight of her with Farid but none were bold enough to approach and speak to him. Farid, for his part, shot glares at everyone.

"Do you normally do this?" she muttered at his side.

"Do what?" he asked as they walked beyond the cells and toward the cages at the end.

"Look at everyone as if you'll crush them."

His steps slowed and Sora shifted her gaze to the right to see his expression. He met her gaze head on. "I don't look at anyone. I don't talk to anyone. On any fight day, I can be scheduled against one of them. It's easier when I have a death match to not have a connection or remembered conversation with an opponent I have to kill."

Sora stopped, stunned by his revelation. Why hadn't she thought of that? She, with cybernetic enhancements in her brain, had completely ignored the toll these fights would take on the contenders. "I'm sorry. You're right."

He nudged her along to continue. "Up here."

They reached the end of the aisle and on her right Kaito and Xion sat on the ground inside their respective cages. Kaito's hair had been neatly brushed and he wore a pair of clean thigh length tight shorts and boots on his feet. Xion, in comparison, was covered in dirt and torn pants. His feet were bare and dirt covered the bottoms.

Other than those minor things, a surface scan didn't show any permanent damage.

"These are two of the new fighters," Farid announced loudly as if she didn't know them.

Kaito was the one scheduled for the death bout. Sora didn't know much about his background. Only that he'd been in the

Cyborg Military Elite and he was a member of Kelix's and Cyllus' pod.

Lunging to their feet, Kaito and Xion glared at Farid. They probably thought he wanted to check out his competition. Drawing their attention, she said in a bored tone, "They don't seem strong. I wonder how long the one will last in his match today. My friend Kelix could probably take them."

Their harsh gazes shifted toward Sora. Moments later, recognition flared. Xion blew out a relieved exhale. Kaito propped his hands on his waist and lowered his head to stare at the floor.

Farid pointed to the cage across the aisle. "That's the opponent he'll be going against."

It hurt to see Zozo's bowed head and hunched over figure as he sat on an upturned crate someone had put in his cage. He really didn't belong in this environment. No one did unless they'd agreed to this and Sora found it hard to believe this gentle, quiet being had volunteered to fight, let alone the death match he was in against Kaito.

"Farid, back so soon, I see."

Beside her, Farid tensed and the hand she'd been holding squeezed hers before he dropped it and turned. "Mizra."

A muscular male dressed in a tan loincloth and ankle high boots lumbered toward them with a broad grin. His gaze latched onto Sora and his steps slowed. The smug look in his eyes turned to one of interest.

When his lips curved upward, Sora stiffened and set her feet in a ready stance. The one called Mizra drew near.

"What do you want?" Farid asked.

The coldness in his voice set off warnings. She'd read the file on Mizra. He'd been here a little over eight years. Besides Tok Su, who'd been here for ten like Farid, Mizra was the next longest residing fighter. Tok Su was still in the medical facility and recovering from his last brutal match where he'd almost died.

What Sora remembered notably about Mizra was the number of death matches he'd been scheduled during his tenure onboard. Farid had over five hundred fights but only a dozen had been to the death. Mizra had a great number of death fights. Almost as if the conglomerate sensed he thrived on them.

Mizra broke his stare from Sora's finally and faced Farid. "I wanted one last look at the Nagani before we enter the arena."

***

To rile the serpent up more than likely. Bindor lay in a coil in his cage but his piercing gaze watched them intently. Farid sneered at Mizra. "Don't let us hold you up."

Mizra glanced at Sora again. "I caught the promo on these two. Wish I'd been paired up to fight one of them. Heard a little rumor that the mark on their faces means they're cyborgs."

"You don't have to wait. Come closer and I'll show you what its like to be pitted against a cyborg," Kaito snarled from behind them.

Malice gleamed from Mizra's eyes as he stepped around Sora to stand in front of Kaito's cage. Proving he wasn't completely stupid, he maintained a sufficient distance in case the cyborg reached through the bars and grabbed him.

"Our time will come, if you survive today." Mizra snorted. "Not like you'll be going anywhere. Whatever life you had before is over."

Sora moved beside him and Farid blocked her with a subtle twist of his body. Her gaze jerked up to his and she glared. He cupped her jaw and leaned over to kiss her softly on the mouth as he whispered, "Do *not* react."

She leaned into his embrace and Farid wished they weren't in full view of others to hold her the way he wanted. Her pain and anger at seeing her friends locked in cages reflected in her gaze. One only had to look at her and see Sora wanted to rip the bars down but they had an electronic component she'd have to disable. In their current circumstances, that would be a huge mistake.

He kept his hand on her face until she reluctantly nodded agreement. Farid waited another minute to be sure she had her control back then eased away. Turning to Mizra, Farid snapped, "Move on!"

Mizra smirked. "I'd say see you in the arena but not sure you'll ever touch those grounds again."

Unwilling to let him draw a response, Farid merely stared. On a huff, and after one last glance at Sora, Mizra went to the cage where the Nagani was held.

Farid kept a careful eye on Mizra as he muttered to Sora, "Speak to them quickly if you need to. We have to move soon before it looks like we spent too much time here."

Kaito's attention flicked to Farid but Farid didn't speak to the cyborg. Sora pretended to gaze around them and lowered her voice. "Kelix is here. We plan to get both of you out."

"Before the fight?" Kaito asked intently.

There was a low hum of something in the tone he used on the question. A fake sneer twisted Sora's lips but she replied lightly, "I can't guarantee it. Too much of the spotlight is on you and the fight. It's also a death match which tends to draw more of a crowd."

She was right. Everyone on the *Gladyx* showed up for the fights billed as gory. The fascination for death would never make sense to Farid.

"Our whereabouts will get back to Shui," Xion said from his cage.

Sora sighed. "I know. Your images were blasted across the *Gladyx* system and there's no telling how many shared it."

"We need to go," Farid cut in, placing his hand over her shoulder and moving her forward.

Kaito offered a chin lift and Xion hurried to whisper, "Let Kelix know we should be in range of our NNP. We've tried and been unable to connect with him."

Farid wouldn't be surprised if the ship ran a signal jammer. Sora walked at his side but anger practically vibrated from her shoulders beneath his arm. He wanted to ask if she was alright yet hesitated as they circled the lower level and made their way toward the entrance they'd used to come in.

"The fights will begin shortly," he said instead. "Do you want to stay or leave?"

She looked up briefly. "I have to stay."

"I'll stay with you." Farid didn't like watching the fights. He'd meant what he said to Sora earlier. Watching the fights wasn't pleasurable for him in anyway. He'd learned the hard way during his first year not to get close to the others, not to watch their fights. It all stemmed from his third match.

When he had to deliver the final blow to a fighter who'd befriended him, Farid had been devastated. Never again he'd promised himself and he hadn't broken his word in over five hundred fights. Until today.

"Are you fine with sitting on the bottom tier? It's near the exit."

And closer to the fighting but Farid understood her reasoning. She needed to be near her friends during his fight.

"It's fine."

Chapter 16

The seats they found were on the bottom row. At Sora's side, Farid's arm over her shoulder grew more and more stiff. He scowled at the stares turned in their direction as they approached and sat down. Murmurs rose in the crowd and guests twisted in their seats to get a good luck and confirm it was indeed him.

For his part, Farid leaned back in his seat until he almost slouched, long legs stretched before him. His other arm braced on the small rest bar to the left, hand dangling over the edge. He retained the arm across her shoulders so she snuggled into his side and placed a hand on his flat abdomen.

His posture exhibited a relaxed state but she felt how taut he held himself. The stares, the conversation generated by his unusual presence here, and most important his lack of a slot in the schedule, all had to drive a hole in his heart. Because at the core of this had been his plan to leave here with his son.

"Are you really okay with being here?" she murmured, resting her head against his shoulder as she gazed at the empty arena floor below.

"I don't trust..." he broke off, heaved a breath and glanced around.

Sora lifted her head and shifted in her seat to scan the crowd as well. Farid's arm tightened on her, keeping her close. The stands were packed. More here today than at the last scheduled fight. "What do you see?"

Though his eyes continued to look around, Farid picked up where he left off. "I don't trust any of this. The conglomerate knows the cyborgs from Kirs are labeled rebels. Yet, they set up that broadcast with your friend's match today, alerting everyone to their identity."

True. Together it showed a distinct lack of care Sora wouldn't have expected from a group who ran an illegal traveling gladiator arena. Her worries increased when Kelix entered with three men she recognized as buyers he'd been working with and getting close to. The group climbed the stairs to the third row behind her and Farid.

"Is Durwin one of you?"

Sora jerked at his question. Had she given something away? "What do you mean?"

Farid tipped his head toward her as if to kiss her temple but spoke against her skin. "Cyborg."

Sora swallowed. She didn't want to reveal Kelix's identity yet she'd asked Farid to help her. He was putting himself in danger if this went sideways so she gave him the truth. "Yes."

He sat back in his seat and gazed back at the empty arena. The overhead speakers played a peppy beat while Garod, Urson and Parson walked in with smiles blazing across their faces.

Garod raised his arms and the music went silent. "Welcome! Welcome! This is the moment we've been waiting for. Tonight's entertainment will..."

Sora tuned into Garod's speech and watched Farid simultaneously. He sat like a rigid statue beside her, lips pressed tight and eyes narrowed to slits. She reached up and clasped the hand on her shoulder. His fingers locked onto hers.

And remained there through the first three fights. On the fourth, Farid sat upright and propped his elbows on his knees, staring straight ahead. Kaito and Zozo's name rang out.

Sora risked a glance up and to the left. Kelix watched as his pod brethren strode in. Zozo's steps lumbered behind, his expression bewildered.

Kaito's fight was the only death match on the schedule. His hands clenched at his side as he waited for Zozo to make a move.

Garod's voice spoke from above. "Hold your excitement, everyone. We have something a little special."

More music piped in and Mizra sauntered in with a cocky smirk. Farid laced his fingers together between his spread thighs. Bindor slivered in on his thick eight-foot tail. His upper body was shirtless and his muscular abs rippled each time he moved. The scales on his torso and along his tail shimmered from deep shades of purple to pale lavender tones on the tip which he held up and shook in warning.

"It's a multi-fight showdown! Last man standing death match," Garod announced.

Standing across from Mizra, Bindor swayed in place and hissed. The crowd surged to their feet and screamed. Garod laughed and it echoed throughout the arena. Thumping sounded as everyone stomped, creating a loud clambering noise that hurt her auditory circuits. Sora palmed her ears and winced.

"Let the fight begin!"

Mizra roared but didn't charge the Nagani, his assigned opponent. He went straight for Zozo, punched the somber figure in the gut then swiped his hand out in a violent chop to Zozo's throat. Zozo gagged and dropped to his knees.

"Wait! Can he do that?" Sora asked in amazement.

Without taking his eyes off of the mayhem, Farid answered, "You can do anything in the arena."

Kaito swung into action and started to attack Mizra but he whirled away and leaped for the Nagani. Sora's heart pounded in her chest and she used her processor to modulate the rhythm. "Why allow this? The bets. The credits."

"The *Gladyx* will profit no matter how this turns out."

Of course they would. The Nagani whipped his tail over Mizra's head and missed. Zozo staggered to his feet and swung at Kaito from behind. The cyborg swung around and led with his fist. Kaito must have put his enhanced strength behind the blow because his arm powered straight through Zozo's midsection up to his elbow.

Gasps rang out. Sora leaped to her feet. As realization dawned, the look on Kaito's face was devastating. It was easy to see he'd expected Mizra behind him. Zozo grabbed Kaito's shoulder but there was nothing he could do.

Tears slipped down Zozo craggy face. He slowly fell to the side, ripping Kaito's hand from his middle. Blood immediately pooled under his body as he sagged to the ground and stilled.

Mizra laughed loudly. "Oh, how unfortunate!"

The audience stood up and cheered. A thirst for more blood glowed on their faces. No one seemed to care that a contender had just died in front of them.

"And now there were three!" Garod called out and chuckled from the speakers.

Kaito roared and launched for Mizra. He needn't have bothered. Bindor coiled his lower half around Mizra and gripped his head between the flat of his palms. Mizra twisted and struggled but once in a Nagani death coil you were done. Mizra's face paled and he screamed.

The sound reverberated around the arena over and over again as the coils flexed and tightened. One rough snap and Bindor broke Mizra's neck.

Quiet. Everyone grew quiet. Shock filled the arena stands as Bindor slowly unwound himself from Mizra's dead body. He dropped to the ground. Only Bindor and Kaito remained.

"Woohoo! What a match. Who would have expected our final two to be these men?"

Kaito's chest rose up and down as he panted. Bindor swayed in place, his forked tongue flicking in the air.

"What are they doing?" Sora muttered.

"Naganis are peaceful. Bindor doesn't belong here. This fight has probably damaged him emotionally. He has no cause to attack Kaito." Anger evident at this turn of events, Farid stood and crossed his arms over his chest.

Kaito made no move to attack. When neither initiated a fight, the cheers in the stands soon turned to frustrated mutters, then yells and boos.

"Start already!"

"What's the hold up?!"

"Fight!"

Sora wasn't sure Kaito would respond. As a soldier, they'd spent their time protecting innocents. Aside from anything done under the misconception Emperor Shui pushed, the Cyborg Elite Military didn't harm those without cause.

This wouldn't end well. As the minutes ticked by, she kept expecting a member of the conglomerate to threaten or cajole but the speakers were silent.

Bindor whispered something and Kaito flinched. Sora replayed it over and over through her auditory system and filtered out the crowd noise until she knew what he'd said. Once she deciphered the words, Sora stilled and her heart rose to her throat.

"Kill me please."

With no warning, Bindor leaped for Kaito. Just launched his serpentine body in the air and landed next to the cyborg.

In a whip like motion, he whirled around Kaito's standing form but didn't coil his body over the other man. The threat was there as Bindor snapped his teeth in Kaito's face. Kaito dodged the move and back flipped away. He stayed in place and nodded his head.

Bindor slivered to the right and swung a fist at Kaito's midsection. Kaito swung back and the Nagani didn't duck. Kaito hadn't used a fraction of his strength in comparison to how hard he'd hit Zozo. The blow struck and Bindor's upper body was thrown backward. He retained his balance and straightened, using his tail for balance.

Bindor's lips curled in a smile and formed a single word. *"Thanks."*

He charged Kaito and Kaito lashed out with a booted foot. The kick was perfectly calculated and completed with the precision of a trained cyborg. It hit Bindor dead center on his temple and he was dead before his body hit the ground.

Kaito grabbed his head and roared. Rage, grief and pain filled the sound. It must have appeared a triumphant display to the audience because they were back on their feet laughing and celebrating while patting each other on the back. Credits would be paid out for the ones who had made bets on the matches.

Sora turned her head to the side and looked up three rows. The buyers with Kelix looked pissed at this unexpected outcome. Kelix, however, stared at his pod brother in dismay, face drawn. Sora looked back at Kaito but he marched toward the arched entry, back ramrod straight.

"Come on. It's over and I want to get out of here." Farid cupped Sora's elbow and steered her from their seats.

While the audience continued to celebrate, oblivious to the dead bodies left behind, they left.

***

Farid said goodbye to Sora at the door to her room and went to his. Behind the closed frame, he slumped against the panel and let his emotions have free reign. Watching today's matches had been difficult. He'd forgotten how different it felt when he wasn't a participant.

Adrenalin, pain and sometimes fear kept what happened around him to a distant blur he'd learned to control through the years. But today, he didn't have the benefit of that emotional shielding and he'd had to fight to stay and not leave as he'd wanted. Every blow, every jeer and each death struck Farid as if he'd been the one down there.

He ran a shaky hand over his hair and pushed up and away from the door. Heading toward his cleansing room, he decided on a cold shower to shake off the horror of watching three individuals die. All for the purpose of entertainment.

The cyborg may have been the last one standing but he'd never be the same again. Farid knew that better than anyone.

Chapter 17

Sora explained everything to Cyllus on the comm. His expression darkened with each detail she shared.

"Kaito doesn't like killing. The death of the this Zozo will stick with him," he told her somberly.

"I'm not sure Kelix is doing much better," Sora added.

Cyllus grimaced. "If they could communicate on our NNP, it would help. Vent, rage, encourage. You said there's a block?"

Sora sank into the cushions of the chair at her table. "Farid believes a jammer is being used. It's not impacting any other means of communication."

"Could be accidental side effect from something else they're doing," Cyllus said. "Tagan and I are on our way. Kelix reported your update. Thanks to the information both of you have supplied, we should arrive in the air space around the Hanass colony some time tonight."

Knowing their friends were on the way lowered some of Sora's stress levels. They couldn't get here soon enough though. Sora wanted off this ship of misery. She wanted the fighters freed and not just Kaito and Xion. Remembering Zozo's tears and seeing the Nagani being forced to fight against his peaceful nature, left her sick.

"What about Garod and the others? In order to bring them down, we can't let them get away with what they've been doing."

Cyllus agreed. "Understood. You know we have to be careful on how we handle this. We can't afford to draw more attention to ourselves and we absolutely can't risk Shui discovering where we've made our new home."

"I know. We have Thalen and Savie to consider." Savie with her human physiology and Thalen's unconscious state put them at a disadvantage if Shui sent mercs after them.

Cyllus must have noted her concern. "Take faith, Sora. We'll do what's right."

They ended the call shortly afterward. Sora took a deep breath. She and Kelix weren't due to meet until later. It wasn't her first time watching the fights but it was the first time she'd known one of the participants personally and her brief meeting with Zozo had also affected her. Nerves jangled and her processors worked overtime to settle them.

Returning to work wasn't an option since she'd completed her tickets for the day. Sora had to do something to distract herself and to wash away the distaste of seeing the death match. She needed to feel useful.

Thoughts of the care center came to mind. Sora wondered if she could track down the person who'd taken care of Farid's son. Maybe get him closure on the details for his peace of mind. The idea planted firmly in her mind, she turned on her heels and left.

Due to the time of day, very few children remained. The woman she'd spoken to didn't appear to be around but there was female wiping down colorful chairs and toys. She noticed Sora in the doorway and the bulging eyes widened.

Sora waggled her fingers. "Hello. I was hoping to speak with the woman in charge."

Relief flashed over her pale blue face. "You mean Ada. She finished for the day. Can I help you with something? Are you here to pick up one of the children? I'm sorry I don't recognize you, I'm new."

"Welcome. I'm fairly new too. My name's Sora and I've been with the *Gladyx* for a few weeks. I work in maintenance repair."

"It's a pleasure to meet someone else new. I'm Calona. I was told many workers come and go onboard but everyone in the care center has been here for a while so I'm the only new one around," Calona volunteered, dropping her cloth and walking toward Sora.

Sora increased the wattage of her smile. "Maintenance is similar. Not a lot of new workers."

"How can I help you?"

"When I spoke to the Ada earlier, she mentioned another caretaker had been reassigned after a long-term assignment and I thought maybe I could speak to her regarding the child she'd been responsible for prior." Sora held her breath and waited.

"You're probably thinking of Chala. At least, I think. She's the only who's ever had a long term assignment and only watches one child. He doesn't have a family. His parents were fighters who died in the arena. She's not reassigned though so maybe I'm mistaken."

Sora's pulse raced. Her brain calculating and recalculating what she'd heard. "The child...do you happen to know his name?"

"Sure. It's Turin."

Sora stumbled back. "What?"

Calona's brows creased. "Are you okay?"

"Fine. Fine." Sora's thoughts flew. Why had she been told Farid's son was dead? What reason would Garod have to lie to her?

"Should I tell her you were here?"

Clearing her throat, Sora met Calona's bemused gaze. "No. That's okay. I had a question but I can come by another time. Thanks for your help and hope you enjoy your journey with the *Gladyx*."

"Alright. Oh, if you want to see Turin, you can have a quick peek. He's never down here but Chala had to run an errand and left him with me for a short bit. We don't usually allow anyone to talk to the children without permission from the parents but with his case, it shouldn't be a problem."

It was too good an opportunity to resist. If she told Farid his son lived without verifying and the child Calona referenced wasn't his son, it would be like reliving the nightmare of Turin's death all over.

"I'd like to see him but only if you won't get in trouble," Sora said.

"Sure. He's on the floor behind me putting away the toys from the other children. He's very responsible and seems awfully quiet for his age. Chala says he suffers from a terrible sickness in his stomach."

Calona leaned a little to the side and Sora could make out the back of a young boy placing items on a shelf and closing the drawer on another carefully. His black hair was pulled back in a short nub at his nape. He wore a gray one-piece jumpsuit cinched at a really narrow waist. His side profile revealed a green face with brown mixed in.

Sora wasn't an expert on Gurzal children but compared to Farid's size, Turin seemed unreasonably thin for an almost ten year old. "You said he suffers from a stomach ailment."

"Yes. Chala said there are days where he can't get out of the bed and that's why he's not allowed in the center. In my short time here today, he's been sick at least three times."

Sora tried to recall if Farid had mentioned Turin being sickly. They hadn't really talked about him though. His pain had been great and Sora figured it was too soon.

Zooming in with her ocular implant, she studied his tiny features. Gurzal came up on her internal display. He could be Farid's son but he could also belong to someone else and they happened to have the same name. The likelihood was slim but she'd already delivered news that his child was dead.

What if she'd been wrong? Having to go back and tell him she'd made a mistake only to find out that this child wasn't actually his...

She'd talk to Kelix. Something wasn't right and Sora wanted to get to the bottom of it before she gave Farid hope then destroyed his world all over again. Seeing such a strong man brought low with his pain once was enough.

The child turned and saw Sora and Calona. He stood and hesitantly approached. His gaze jumped from Sora and back to Calona. When he neared, Calona went to her knees and tipped her head to the side. "What is it, Turin?"

"Who is she?"

His voice was quiet. So low Sora might have missed it if she hadn't been enhanced. Calona smiled up at Sora. "I'm sorry. What was your name again?"

Familiar hazel eyes lifted to watch her. Long lashes fluttered as he waited for her to speak. He stood like one who'd been disappointed time and again, shoulders curved waiting for the next blow.

"Sora. I'm Sora."

"Are you a fighter?" he asked her directly.

Would her answer help or hinder? Did he know his father was a fighter? Farid mentioned getting updates but he hadn't seen Turin since he was extremely young. It was hard to gauge if his son would remember him. Sora couldn't imagine what story they'd given the child or if they'd bothered to explain why suddenly stopped seeing his father face to face.

"No. I work in maintenance. I get to fix things."

He offered a hesitant grin and the slash of dimples in his cheeks hit her heart. When he smiled he looked like a miniature replica of Farid. Or was she seeing what she wanted?

Sora ran probability scans, examined every feature and the result was in the ninetieth percentile that the child she was told had died, actually lived and stood before her.

Farid's son.

"I know about maintenance techs and the repair team. I like talking to Kellina and Kaylen when they come to work on the vid screen in my rooms. I want to fix things like they do when I grow up," he said, taking a bold step toward Sora.

She hadn't entered the care center, remaining in the doorway but in another few steps, Turin would be in touching distance. As if realizing that, Calona stood and made an awkward gesture with her hands. "I'm sorry. I don't believe I'm supposed to let the children talk to anyone unless it's a parent or an approved visitor."

"I understand. I only stopped by because I had a minute after the fights today."

From the corner of her eyes, Turin perked up. Sora pretended not to notice and continued to chat with Calona, building a rapport that might prove beneficial later.

Calona brushed her hands nervously down the front of her pants. The camaraderie they'd established was there but nerves were kicking in. "Well, I should finish closing things down. Chala will arrive shortly for Turin."

"It was great meeting you." With a little wave, Sora turned to leave.

"Did you know my father?" Turin called out suddenly.

Sora froze. Everything in her said to continue as if she hadn't heard but the sounds of Farid's despair, the way he'd sobbed in her arms—she had to discover the truth, but risking Turin wasn't an option either. Casually, she glanced over her shoulder. "Does he work in maintenance?"

Disappointment tipped his mouth downward and he scuffed his foot on the floor. Sighing heavily, he ducked his head. "Never mind."

Calona gripped his shoulder and Sora gave one last smile before leaving. Some urge, some bit of feeling she couldn't explain had her saying to Turin. "If you need anything ask for Sora. I'm in the maintenance tech directory."

He didn't look up or acknowledge her.

***

After the fights, Farid was at a loss. He'd tried eating, sleeping, working out. None of it helped. Restless energy plagued his senses with no way to expend the emotion building up. So many things were on his mind. Turin. His schedule.

Fuck his schedule.

Without his son, there was no reason to keep doing Garod's bidding. Farid could leave the *Gladyx*, see if there could be more to his connection to Sora. If she even wanted to spend time with him after she rescued her cyborg friends.

Late into the night, he finally gave up on sleep. He dressed in the dark and left his rooms with the intent to head to the soaking rooms but his steps led him to another level and another room. Standing in front of Sora's door, Farid took a deep breath and knocked.

Time ticked by and it hit him that she could be sleep. Just because he was up didn't mean she'd had any difficulty falling to sleep.

As he turned to leave, the door opened, revealing Sora's slim figure clad in a black short sleeve shirt and tight black shorts. The muscular lines of her legs drew his gaze, flexing as she shifted her stance on bare feet. The smallest feet he'd ever seen.

"Farid?"

He swiped a hand down his face and shoved his hands in his pants pockets. "Can I come in?"

She looked up and down the hall before answering. "Of course. Is everything okay?"

Hair tousled and a small crease on her right cheek, her half-sleepy appearance was a balm to his dark mood. He entered. "I didn't mean to wake you. Time got away from me and I didn't realize how late it was."

"Mmm. Come on." She gestured down the hall and Farid followed.

She led them to her bedroom and climbed into the pulled back sheets, patting a spot on the bed next to her.

"Sora, look." Farid blew out a breath and tugged at his hair. "I'm not sure why I'm here. I'll go."

"Get in the bed, Farid."

The command acted like a shot to his groin and his cock stood at attention. The desire for sex was there but Farid wasn't sure he actually wanted to have sex tonight.

Tugging his shirt over his head and kicking off his shoes, he climbed into her bed and settled on his side next to her. "I need to hold you, touch you."

Sora laid her head down on her folded arms. "The fights really bother you?"

Farid curved an arm around her waist and pulled their fronts together. He tucked her head beneath his jaw and admitted a truth he hadn't spoken to anyone else. "I hate them. I hate being in them and I hate watching them."

Chapter 18

Guilt ate at Sora. After getting in the bed with her, Farid had gone quiet and not spoken a single word since. She lay nestled in his warm arms and all she could think of was what she'd learned a short while ago. His son lived.

It was her fault for telling him different. She'd created part of this emotional turmoil he was under. And why?

Because she'd been desperate to find a way to convince Farid to her side. Instead of researching the words of a stranger, she'd taken them for truth with no evidence and run straight to Farid to sway him. She'd had sex with him.

Sora stilled. If Farid learned the truth, he'd think she did it to make him believe her, to hide the lie she'd told. Except she hadn't known it was a lie. There had been nothing in Ada's voice inflection, her eye movement had remained consistent and her poise stayed lax.

Whatever secret the conglomerate had, the woman she'd spoken with believed one hundred percent Turin had died and what she'd told Sora was the truth.

Farid ran a hand down the slope of Sora's back and spoke, breaking the extended silence. "You okay? You're tense."

She nervously cleared her throat and pressed a tender kiss to the base of his throat. "I'm fine. Just a bit tired."

A caress brushed the roots of her hair, his fingers gliding softly over the top then settling back at the base of her spine. "I didn't mean to wake you by showing up at your door in the middle of the night."

He apologized. Again. If what she'd discovered ended up being true, Sora was the one who'd owe him an apology. She shook her head and patted the side of his hip. "Don't worry about that. I sleep easily."

When she didn't have a lot on her mind. Like now. Final confirmation had come through. Tonight was the night. Preparations had been made for a distraction and Cyllus was on his way. As soon as Kelix contacted her, she'd have to get dressed and move quickly. The plan entailed grabbing Kaito and Xion then fleeing the *Gladyx* in emergency tubes which Cyllus would pull into the ship he piloted.

Farid continued to stroke her back over her tee shirt and Sora leaned into the touch. Being with him like this gave her a sense of security she only felt when surrounded by her pod members. Those men had relied on her in life and death situations and vice versa. Thalen especially being close to her since childhood and willing to threaten anyone who looked at her wrong.

"What will you do when you leave here?"

Farid's whispered question caught her off-guard. Her identity on the cruiser was purely made up. Neither of them had touched on anything personal. They'd shared their bodies, not their minds. Yet, Sora knew a part of her wanted more from Farid.

"I'm still searching for the others from my pod. I guess we'll regroup on the base we've established and figure our next step. Once we save Kaito and Xion, Kelix's pod will be complete but the others have friends missing too. Same as me."

Farid hummed under his breath, another press of his lips to her temple. Sora blinked back the burn building behind her lids. Why was he so gentle? The life he'd lived these last ten years should have hardened him.

"Are you still planning to free your friends tonight?" he asked next.

Sora considered how to answer. She and Kelix didn't trust anyone on the *Gladyx* for obvious reasons. Farid was different. They'd intentionally sought a fighter to give them insight into the conglomerate. Though Farid didn't learn much they hadn't already known, Sora had the strong feeling he wouldn't betray them.

"Yes. Our friends are on their way as we speak with a ship we'll transfer to and keep going."

The arm curved above their heads on the pillow stiffened, the one hand rubbing her back paused in motion then continued. Sora waited for him to voice his concern or explain what had caused the change in him. Hushed silence whispered back. Unable to resist her need to know, the question bubbled forth. "What?"

He didn't make her wait, responding right away. "Did you mean what you said about taking down the *Gladyx*? Are you still planning to help me kill Garod?"

There was no accusation in the roughly voiced questions. Just calm acceptance of whatever she chose to answer. After learning what she had in the care center, Sora wanted to kill Garod more than ever for this game he played with Farid's life.

"Oh, he definitely needs to die. We'll be coming back to finish the job once we have the others safe."

Farid pushed up to his elbow on one side and cupped her jaw. His gaze glowered. "Don't risk yourself out of some misguided form of obligation to me, Sora. It won't bring Turin back. When you get away, don't look back, don't return. Garod and the others in the conglomerate are dangerous. There's a reason they've never been stopped or caught by the authorities."

Sora sat up also and shifted about to fold her legs on the side beneath her. His worry for her touched that secret place in her heart she thought dead and buried. The knowledge she held of his son soured in her stomach and she feared she'd be ill all over the sheets.

She had to tell him. Even if there was a slim possibility it was a mistake. He deserved to know there was hope. She touched his thigh. "Farid..."

He clasped her hand in his and held it between them. "Before you say anything, promise you won't try to track the *Gladyx* and come back."

She refused to agree to that. She would see this enterprise brought down. Taking a deep breath, Sora plunged forward with what she'd learned. "I think Tur—"

Her encrypted comm she'd retrieved from the floor boards buzzed. Kelix. Damn it. She couldn't ignore this. "Farid, I have to tell you something. It's important. But I have to answer this."

She waited for his nod of agreement, tossed her pillow aside and answered her comm. "Talk to me."

"It's done."

Kelix didn't have to say anything else. His words confirmed he'd set the shockwave bombs that would provide the distraction they needed to break Kaito and Xion out of their cages.

"How long?"

"You've got five minutes to meet me in the lower level behind the arena before this place is lit like a celebration."

"Right. I'm on my way." Sora disconnected and tossed the comm as she rolled out of bed.

Farid did the same and stood patiently while she pulled on her pants and jammed her feet into a pair of boots. "What can I do to help, Sora?"

"Stay safe." The answer rolled easily off her tongue because that's what she wanted for Farid. Him, safe.

His hazel eyes narrowed and the similarity to Turin's made her flinch, throwing a torquing wrench into her need to remain disconnected and focused.

"I'm going with you."

Based on his set features and the stubborn lines around his eyes, to argue would be pointless. Grabbing her comm, she hurried into the living area and bent beside the main wall across from the door. She dug her fingers into the sides to pry the panel for electrical components away. It wouldn't budge. "Fuck!"

No time to dawdle. Her internal timer had started a countdown from the moment she ended the call with Kelix. Three minutes then everything went boom. Sora stood and smashed her boot into the wall. The pieces splintered, bits falling to the floor.

Inside, were the two weapons Kelix had smuggled to her and a mini comms ear piece. Destroying the handheld comm was easy and she used the adhesive to stick the mini behind her ear.

Next, Sora reached for the knife inside and tucked it into her waistband, the rapid fire laser she kept in a comfortable grip in her hand. On the way to the door, she said, "Farid, this is dangerous. Everything's going to happen really fast right now. The explosives, our friends arriving. Let Garod believe you a lover betrayed. You can't risk him knowing you had anything to do with helping me."

She opened the door, prepared to dart through. Farid reached over her head and smacked his palm on the frame, closing it. Pushing forward until he had her back pressed against the flat of the door, he leaned in and kissed her. A hard, quick connecting of their mouths. An instant later, he dropped his arm and moved away. "I'm staying with you until I see you've made it away safely."

Urgency was the key. Two minutes. Sora nodded. This time, Farid opened the door before her and they marched out together.

***

Farid wasn't sure what he was thinking only that he wasn't ready to let Sora out of his sight. He'd been so set on avoiding a relationship of any kind until he had more to offer a woman. Now, with the possibility of her leaving in front of him, his heart clamored for more time.

More time to get to know her. More time to discover her secrets.

Seeing Sora move down the hall with laser focus intrigued him and increased his worry in equal measure. Yes, she was a cyborg with incredible strength, but it did nothing to ease his mind. He'd seen stronger beings get taken down in the arena due to a simple error in judgment, a slight miscalculation. Anyone could die.

A knot formed in the pit of his stomach. Like...his son. Hurt and anger clamored for attention. Farid shoved the emotions down. Not now. Later.

They cleared the levels of the ship without running into anyone. All was quiet at this late hour and no one was about. Sora's stride picked up and soon she was racing down the hall. Her stamina impressed Farid and he had to push himself to keep up.

He recognized the maintenance area as she turned the final corner and went straight to a wall mounted comp station. Standing next to it, she pulled a cord free and jammed it straight into her right eye.

"Sora!" he hissed in surprise and fear.

She held up a hand for silence. The gray orb darkened then turned bright red. "I can absorb energy from here. This is the fastest way for me to power up and take the cameras offline. I don't have time to hack the system."

The red pupil flashed a few times before going gray again. Sora yanked the cord away and tossed it to the side. Farid flinched at her rough handling but she was on the move again, this time leading them to the door of the fighting area where the cells and cages were.

"It's locked after fights," he offered, hoping she wouldn't jam anything in her eyes again or somewhere else. There was a thin trickle of blood at the inside corner from where she'd scratched her eyelid.

Sora tossed him a grin as she studied the security panel to the right of the door. "Not a problem for me, remember?"

She placed her palm completely over the square plaque and narrowed her gaze. Within seconds sparks flickered and white lights sparked around her fingers. Then a low beep sounded.

Stunned, Farid stared. So many questions came to mind. Could all cyborgs do that? He'd never met any beings with cybernetic upgrades, the process extreme and complex. Plus, he and Sora hadn't talked about that part of her.

Not enough time. They hadn't had nearly enough time to learn one another. Until now, he hadn't wanted to know anyone but he wanted to know about Sora.

She waved him forward and walked through the sliding door the moment it opened, heading directly for the cages where they'd seen the two cyborg men. Farid stayed close to guard her back. The other fighters in this area were sleep. All except Bommba, the Doorian. He rested on his back and watched them.

When they reached the end of the aisle, the two cyborgs stood at the bars of their individual cages, eyes locked on Sora's approach.

"Hurry," Xion said.

Repeating whatever process she'd done to the outer door, Sora soon had the locks on their cages fried and the bars parted with a mechanical click.

"We've got one minute to haul ass," Sora muttered.

Xion shot from his cage while Kaito moved slower, his gaze no less sharp. Farid recognized the look on his face. Killing for survival as he'd probably done in his role as a soldier was one thing, doing it against your will for the entertainment of others was another.

It took a lot of years to build walls to learn how to deal with the emotional damage that caused. Kaito met his stare and his brows drew tight together. "What's he doing here?"

Already moving back toward the entrance, Sora spoke over her shoulder. "Helping. I don't know you beyond what Cyllus and Kaito have shared but Farid is helping me at great risk to himself."

Xion grunted and scanned the area. "Any more weapons?"

"No. It was hard for Kelix to get me these but here." She tossed the knife through the air toward him. Turning to Kaito, she handed off the laser. Both looked at her in some surprise. "You know what I can do."

Though Farid had no idea what she referenced, knowledge flickered in the gazes of the other men and they nodded. Sora pressed a finger to the small comms she had attached behind her ear. "Kelix, they're out. We're heading to the docking bay."

Chapter 19

Sora arrived in the docking bay right on time. Yellow lights above switched on and a computerized voice from the sound system spoke. "Please be advised that section C through E are off-limits. Minor explosions detected. Repair crew en route."

She flashed a wicked grin at Farid who appeared confused. Sora drew close to his side, her eyes on the others. She touched his wrist. "Thank you, Farid. For everything. You need to go now."

The corner of his mouth lifted. "I didn't do much. You and your friend had everything in hand."

He'd been more than helpful. "You helped us confirm Kaito and Xion's presence."

A huff slipped free and he squeezed her hand lightly. "You would have discovered it when the announcement of the fight was shared."

"But knowing sooner enabled us to get our other friends enough warning to get here. The *Gladyx* travels a lot to keep anyone like the authorities from being able to catch up to them. There is a ship closing in right now with current coordinates to get us away. *You* helped make that happen with your efforts whether you view them as small or not."

Another sigh, rougher as Farid held her gaze and tucked a stray curl behind her ear. "From the first moment I met you, you've been passionate about your promises."

She didn't know where he was going with this and cupped her hand over his. "I don't say things I don't plan on doing."

"And no matter what I said earlier, you still intend to return and make sure Garod and the conglomerate are taken down, don't you?"

The wry twist to his lips warned her not to bother lying. She and Kelix had the evidence they needed to plant seeds that would soon flourish. Not to mention six cyborgs on a common mission could cause a lot of damage.

"It has to be done. I made a promise to you," she vowed.

His fingers traced over her cheekbones. "Sora, I don—"

Frightened by whatever he might say while adrenalin spiked in both of them, Sora cut him off. She had her own things to say. One important thing. "Farid, about your s—"

"Eyes up!" Kelix burst through, running into the docking bay. He held two lasers and fired blasts behind him. "I might have tipped my hand when I slit the throat of a buyer who admitted to sexually abusing fighters for a small fee with permission from the conglomerate."

Broad grins stretched over Xion and Kaito's faces as Kelix threw both lasers in the air toward them, then withdrew two more from the back of his waist.

"We can hear you," Xion announced, the relief visible on his face at having the private intimate form of communication back with his pod brother.

Sirens trilled above. Kelix stopped beside Sora, glanced at Farid then back to her. "Can you do that thing you do but lock the doors instead of opening them? Security was hot on my heels."

"Of course." Heart racing, Sora kissed Farid. "Go!"

"Sora—"

Whatever he was about to say, she knew she couldn't hear it now. Her heart already felt torn. A painful goodbye would hurt. "Go, Farid! Please!"

His lips firmed before he nodded abruptly and took off running in the opposite direction and an emergency exit. Sora went to the large double doors Kelix had come in through and placed the tip of one finger on the ID cam. Sparks flew and the entry light turned red. Going a step further, she moved toward several electro panels controlling the power to this section of the ship.

"Fuck, yes!" Kelix suddenly crowed. "Cyllus is in range. I can hear him through our NNP."

The rush and thrill of action filled Sora then her gut clenched as she recalled Turin. She hadn't told Farid what she'd discover. She looked around the bay and the shuttle crafts. He was no longer in sight. Because she'd sent him away. "Damn it!"

Kelix signaled her. "Sora, Cyllus says he sees the *Gladyx*. We need to get into the emergency tubes. He's got the tractor beam ready to pull us in the moment he sights them."

Thunderous booms slammed into the door, jerking their attention toward it. The buzzer sounded repeatedly as the guards tried using their codes to get in. Sora focused back on the panels in front of her and pressed her palm down on the surface. She closed her eyes and thought of what she wanted to power down.

"Get Xion and Kaito out of here," she instructed.

Between the three men, they maneuvered four emergency tubes on the track that would launch them through a shaft out of the ship and into space. While they got those ready, she turned back to her task.

Taking vital parts of the systems offline wasn't her goal. Only slow the engines, lock the few weapons her processors sensed and undo the access overrides.

For every code Sora managed to shut down, she could tell a tech immediately tried to reestablish the connection. Whoever was on the other end was good. Very good.

"Ah, ah," she whispered. As a cyborg, her skills were above average, with the added gift of the energy she controlled, no way could an ordinary being match her.

Behind her, an emergency tube shot out the chute. One down. Another powered up.

"Sora! Let's go," Kelix shouted.

"Just a sec." One last thing. A single thought sent through the ship's network and the computer allowed her to leave an embedded secondary tracker beacon. She rose and turned.

"Hurry." Kelix waited impatiently beside three remaining slender tubes. Emergency use only was stamped in bright red letters on the top. Xion climbed into one, laid on his back and the lid snapped shut, leaving her to assume Kaito had been in the first to launch.

Turin. A vision of the quiet child with the hazel eyes asking if she knew his father flashed into her mind. Sora couldn't leave without telling Farid. She couldn't. "I needed to tell Farid something."

"There's no time, Sora. We can contact him after we get Xion and Kaito settled," Kelix said.

"Oh, I'm sure there's plenty of time for Sora to share what she wants."

The voice had them spinning in unison. Boots clacked ominously. Garod stepped from between two shuttles and entered the open court of the docking bay. Sora's upper lip curled. Seeing him after the discovery of Farid's son being alive, the lie with the caretaker for whatever reason...

Rage took over and if she'd still had a weapon in hand, Sora would have fired point blank and killed him. Forget the plan, forget destroying the conglomerate and stopping the *Gladyx*.

"You are evil," she sneered. "Farid didn't deserve your lies."

"I'm not the one who lied to get what I wanted," Garod said and made a tsking sound. "My arrangement with Farid was clear and straight forward. Right, Farid?"

Three guards appeared, leading Farid between them. The hair at the nape of Sora's neck curled. She didn't understand what was going on and why Farid hadn't gone back to his rooms. Eyeing Garod in distaste, Sora snarled, "I've never lied to Farid."

Garod laughed out loud. "The truth will be revealed."

Cyllus voice whispered through the comm at her ear. "I've got Kaito. Send out the next. You all have to hurry. The *Gladyx* sent out a distress call. Notices and flags are popping up left and right about deadly cyborgs attacking a vessel."

Kelix smashed his hand on the release atop the emergency tube and it shot along the track and out the chute, sending Xion to Cyllus and safely away just as another individual walked out and joined Garod.

Sora automatically catalogued her appearance. Rich brown skin, large pointed ears on top of a head covered with thick black hair pulled up in a knot. Her diamond shaped eyes flickered in every direction.

Holding her hand was a small thin child. Garod placed a firm hand on the boy's shoulder and his smile widened. Farid's reaction whipped at Sora's guilt. He wore a stunned expression. "Turin?"

Turin didn't lift his gaze from the floor in front of him. Remorse tightened Sora's chest. "I was going to tell you, Farid."

When he glanced at Sora, the look in his eyes was of utter betrayal. She swallowed and took a step toward him. Weapons powered up and the guards next to Garod aimed the ends of their lasers at her.

"You knew?" Farid asked.

He wasn't supposed to learn about his son here. Not like this. "Farid, I can explain."

***

Farid had told himself to leave as Sora directed and return to his rooms. He could pretend a lack of knowledge of her actions if asked. Except his mind and heart wouldn't let him. He crouched near a shuttle and planned to remain there until she got off the *Gladyx* safely.

If anyone tried to stop her, Farid was an excellent fighter. A grim smile twisted his lips. He'd welcome a fight right now. For once, he had hope. Something would finally stop the *Gladyx* and their business of blackmailing and forcing individuals into the fight ring.

He didn't fool himself into thinking others wouldn't replace the system the conglomerate had created. Legal arena fights weren't considered nearly as exciting and didn't have death matches.

Where there was a need, others would find a way. No matter the cost, no matter who was injured in the process. But for Farid, he wanted to watch this particular group burn. Sora would keep her word. She'd find a way to reach him when the time came.

The cyborgs worked to get several emergency tubes lined up for their escape. He focused so hard on her ease with the three men, he never heard a thing until something jammed against the side of his head and a voice roughly demanded, "Get up."

Farid slowly stood and faced three armed guards, including the one who had his laser pointed at his temple, and a gloating Garod. The other two members of the conglomerate weren't present but he knew they had to be aware of everything going on in the docking bay. Nothing onboard got past their notice.

"Hold him here." Garod gestured to the one aiming his weapon at Farid then moved toward the open area where Sora and her friends were.

Farid strained to hear what was said.

"You are evil," Sora snapped. "Farid didn't deserve your lies."

What lies? Had she discovered something?

"I'm not the one who lied to get what I wanted," Garod said and made a tsking sound. "My arrangement with Farid was clear and straight forward. Right, Farid?"

The guards surrounded Farid and shoved him forward. He considered disarming them but couldn't be certain Sora and the cyborgs wouldn't get caught in the crossfire. One of the four tubes they'd set out was gone. Best to bide his time and wait for the right moment to aid them.

Sora's rigid posture drew his attention. "I've never lied to Farid."

Garod laughed out loud, the sound chilling Farid with the note of triumph in it. "The truth will be revealed."

New steps rang out and another person joined them. A woman. Holding her hand was a small child. Garod placed a firm grip on the boy's shoulder and his smile widened.

Blood drained from Farid's face and the ground shifted beneath his feet. His heart skipped a beat then pounded out a driving rhythm. He studied the slim frame of the boy, the shock of black hair falling over his smooth brow. His mottled green and brown skin wasn't as vibrant as it should have been for a Gurzal and he seemed unnaturally thin for one of their race.

The angle of the child's bent head only allowed Farid to see his profile but it was enough. There was no doubt in his mind who he was staring at. Joy exploded in his chest. Happiness, relief, fear. "Turin?"

Turin didn't lift his gaze from the floor in front of him.

"I was going to tell you, Farid," Sora whispered

When he glanced in her direction, remorse darkened her gray eyes to that of an approaching storm cloud. She swallowed and took a step toward him. Weapons powered up and the guards next to Garod aimed their lasers at her.

"You knew?" Farid asked in a choked voice. He couldn't move. His gaze greedily took in the first sight of his son in five years. Why wouldn't she have told him? No, she'd said Turin was *dead*.

She shook her head back and forth. "Farid, I can explain. I needed more time. Come with us and I'll explain everything"

"I'm afraid that won't be possible. Farid owes us two more fights and *you* won't be going anywhere either."

As soon as Garod spoke, he signaled the guards.

"Sora!" the buyer, Durwin, yelled.

Sora caught the laser he flung her way and fired but someone beat her to it. Shots rang out, knocking each laser from the hands of the guards. Their weapons fell to the floor with a clatter as they cried out and grabbed their singed fingers.

Sora turned toward the newcomer who came through the main door as if it hadn't been locked. Farid studied the tall man striding toward them with confidence. The high collared, all black suit identified him as a buyer. Orange skin puckered and drew tight over his unibrow. Deep set eyes narrowed as he sneered at Garod. "Don't threaten a cyborg. You have no idea of what we're capable."

"Kona?" Durwin gaped, naming another buyer Farid had heard of but never seen.

Kona reached up and peeled back the edges of his face. Not his face, an extensive latex covering. Beneath it was smooth tanned skin and a CR brand high on his cheek.

Another cyborg? Farid had no idea what was going on.

"Reo!" Sora gasped.

Garod glared and spoke faster. "This woman lied to you, Farid. She tricked you to get your help. She said your son was dead to get you to work against us to free her friends. She didn't care about you. Women never do. They only want the pleasure of sleeping with an arena fighter."

Each accusation stabbed at Farid's soul.

Chapter 20

"Farid, please. None of this was a planned trick."

"Drop your weapon!" Garod demanded as if Sora would actually listen.

"You're not in control here anymore, Garod," Reo drawled.

Sora couldn't believe he was here. Questions pounded at her brain but now wasn't the time. She could barely look at Farid. Regret churned her stomach into knots. His brows furrowed as he took in everything Garod said.

"Get down, now!" Kelix ordered.

The guards dropped to their fronts on the floor immediately. The caretaker hesitated, shifted her gaze around before slowly folding to her knees then her stomach. Garod screamed. Then to Sora's surprise, Turin broke away from his lax grip and ran.

Straight toward her.

"Turin!" Farid called, his arm outstretched as if to catch hold of the boy.

Turin slammed into Sora's legs and wrapped his arms around her thighs. "I don't want to stay here. You said if I need you to reach out."

His words stabbed at her heart with the same force as his father's glare. She rested a hand on his head and brushed the black waves back. His face lifted up to her and tears glistened in his hazel eyes.

"You both need to hurry and get off that ship! Like now!" Cyllus snapped through the ear comm.

Her glance went to Kelix and he watched her as well. Reo spoke first. "Are the others here too?"

Sora grinded her teeth together and forced herself to unlock her jaw. There would be time later to blast him with the edge of her tongue. "Yes. We have a ship waiting. An emergency call went out stating cyborgs were attacking. Every hunter, pirate and mercenary looking to claim the bounty on us is probably on the way."

Reo snorted. His glance fell to Garod then back to Kelix and Sora. "Get in the tubes. I'll keep this one occupied while you get on your way."

Kelix's expression darkened, "What?! No! You have to come with us."

Reo shook his head before Kelix finished speaking. His eyes glittered with excitement. This was the most lively she'd seen him since hearing the news of his entire pod dying. "I'm closer to finding the two women. They were on the *Gladyx* briefly but got off before I managed an adequate cover to arrive here."

Turin continued to shake and cling to her legs. Sora's processors worked over time to slow her racing heart. Farid took a step toward her, his gaze on his son.

"Don't, Farid!" Garod withdrew a slim black box from his pants pocket and waved it threateningly at Farid. "You won't get out of here alive. I swear!"

Against her legs, Turin jerked. His head lifted and he glanced over his shoulders. "Papa?"

Farid stood rigid, hands clenched at his sides. He met Sora's gaze with rage burning in his eyes. "Take him and leave."

Her mouth fell open. "Wh—"

"Take my son and leave!" he roared. "You owe me that."

Sora bent down and swept the boy up in her arms, his weight neglible, though he started to struggle. "Papa! Papa!"

Garod screamed obscenities. The guards and the caretaker on the ground didn't dare move.

"Come on, come on. We have Kaito and Xion onboard. Ships in range arriving hot and heavy soon. We need to leave. It's now or never," Cyllus barked in her ear.

Spinning around, Sora leaped for one of the open tubes and lay on her back inside, gripping Turin tight. He was full on crying and kicking now. Kelix cursed and jumped into the other tube. Sora managed to see the lid close on his and then her own lid started to close. She caught it with a palm of one hand to the edge, while her other forearm locked over Turin's chest.

"Where will you be, Reo? I'm not leaving unless we have a way to stay in touch with you." She refused to lose track of him again.

He stared down at her, his eyes revealing a sudden spark of gratitude. "I'll send my contact information in an encoded message."

She pinned him with her gaze. "Don't lie or I will hunt you down."

He grinned and pushed her hand away, allowing the lid to close, obscuring her vision. A thump sounded above as Reo hit the launch release on the outside. The tube vibrated beneath her. Sudden pressure jammed her to the side but not once did she let go of Turin.

Within seconds, the tube jolted. The tractor lock. The tube's trajectory smoothed out and then rocked and hit something. Turin sniffled in her arms. She brushed at his hair. “It’s okay. You’re okay.”

Why had Farid told her to take the boy? The lid above opened and Cyllus’ grinning face peered down at her. His gaze shifted to Turin and his smile dropped. “Who—”

“Not now,” she said, sitting up carefully with Farid’s son cradled in her arms.

His limbs were long, hinting at the height he’d one day have. Cyllus reached in and gripped Sora’s forearms. Cyborg strength enabled him to lift her from the tube while she still held onto Turin. Kelix, Xion and Kaito stood together, hugging one another. Though they weren’t speaking, their intense stance hinted at internal communication.

“Shouldn’t you be over there?” she asked Cyllus as he slowly released his hold.

He tapped his temple. “NNP. I’m listening and talking with them now.”

Right. She shifted Turin on her hips and wrapped her arms around his waist to secure his weight. His legs dangled halfway down her own. “This is Turin. I think we need a medic to make sure he’s fine.”

Cyllus nodded. “We’ll be back on Solus in a few hours. We escaped before anyone hoping to collect the bounty on us arrived. The cloaked mode Tagan paid to upgrade this ship is working at peak efficiency and they won’t be able to trace our path.”

“Good.”

Sora still didn’t know what to do next. Cyllus seemed to read her mind and said, “Do you want me to run a quick scan on him now?”

"Yes," Sora breathed out and lowered Turin.

She could have run the scan herself but she didn't trust her clarity in the moment. Farid thought she'd lied to betray him then turned around and sent her away with his son. She wasn't sure how to interpret his actions.

Cyllus squatted in front of Turin. The boy straightened and faced him but one hand clenched tight to Sora's pant leg. She'd never met a child his age so clingy. Kirsian children ran around free and independence was encouraged in all the ones she'd met. Thoughts of what could have happened to him to cause such a reaction made her blood boil.

Kelix came over, Xion and Kaito following. Kelix eyed Turin. "Is everything okay?"

A frown pierced Cyllus' brow. "His core stats are fine but I'm picking up something I can't place or identify."

"Let me," Xion moved in front of Turin who shied away. The other cyborg met Turin's stare. "I know you're afraid of us but it's important that we make sure you're not hurt in anyway."

Turin pushed off of Sora's leg. "Do you know my father?"

It was the same question he'd asked Sora. Did he not...remember Farid?

"Not really. I saw him though," Xion offered with a half smile.

"Chala said he's dead."

Sora flinched and dropped to a crouch to grab Turin by his shoulders. "What?!"

Tears welled in Turin's eyes. "She said he died in a fight but you smelled like him when you came to the care center. In the docking bay there was another Gurzal and everyone called him Farid too. That was my papa's name. He promised we'd live together one day. Like a real family."

Cyllus signaled Xion to do the scan while Turin talked and received a nod in return. Sora squeezed Turin's thin shoulders. "Your father is not dead. He was there in the bay with us. I don't know why you were told that and I'm really sorry you had to deal with it."

Turin sniffed and aggressively wiped the single tear from his face. "Can he come now? I miss him so much. He's been gone a really long time."

Xion whistled under his breath. Cyllus, Kelix and Kaito all froze. Their eyelids fluttered once in the only sign they gave that they communicated silently with one another. Cyllus kept his voice casual as he said, "Sora, we need you to do that special thing you do. Left wrist, right now!"

Sora didn't question Cyllus. She shifted one hand to Turin's wrist and closed her fingers around it. She sensed what they'd discovered at the same moment she shot a jolt of electric current into Turin. He jumped but didn't make a sound, only gave her a puzzling look.

She offered him a wane smile. "Don't worry. Energy manipulation is a little specialty of mine. Had to get rid of a nasty bug you were carrying around with you. All good now."

There had been a remote accessible explosive embedded in Turin's wrist. It had to have been there for a while because tissue and muscle had fused to parts of it. It would have been a difficult surgical process to remove it if anyone ever tried.

She wasn't sure what the range on the device was and it didn't matter. No one should walk around with a bomb inside of them. Especially a child. The electric current she used had fried the wires. They would look into permanent removal on Solus.

No wonder Farid had asked her to take his son. He had to have considered this. Did he have one too? Her heart dropped at the thought. She'd left him behind with Garod.

***

Farid's heart raced. Turin was alive. He couldn't believe it. He didn't doubt for a moment someone had led Sora to believe his son had died. She wouldn't have lied about something like that no matter what Garod tried to imply. Not even to gain his help.

"I'll be on my way."

The unknown cyborg who'd been masquerading as a buyer tossed a cocky salute in their direction. He wore a transponder belt and fiddled with the dial on the front. The next moment, his form vanished.

Garod screamed. "Find him!"

The guards scrabbled to their feet. Farid wished them good luck. Sora's cyborg compatriot could be anywhere on the ship and obviously had access to synthetic facial coverings. He could be disguised as a member of the conglomerate for all they knew.

"You think you've done something!" Garod faced Farid, eyes bulging and flushed a vivid red. He turned to the hovering guards who hadn't moved, growled and whipped out his comm from his pocket. Words flew from his mouth in a garbled snarl. "Find out where the other ship went. Get tech support to bring the systems back online."

Parson and Bindor ran through the open door into the docking bay. Out of breath, Bindor stopped inside to place his hands on his knees and panted. Parson looked around and gasped, "What in blazing stars is going on?"

"There were cyborgs undercover on the *Gladyx*. They stole our new contestants," Garod spat.

Surprise flashed over Bindor's creased features. "But how? What about the explosives?"

The sneer on Garod's face sent a chill down Farid's spine. "We hadn't had a chance to implant them in the two cyborg fighters. Their cybernetics made them resistant to our usual array of drugs to subdue them for the procedure.

Garod spun around and glared at Farid. "We were successful in the other subject though."

The other subject? In an instant, rage blinded Farid. Charging for Garod, he lifted the male high in the air by his shirt and shook him. "What have you done to Turin?!"

Garod laughed and held up his hand with the comm, he flicked an icon and Farid recognized the glowing red symbol. Garod had waved it in his face after he woke in the medical facility, a mere two days after he'd signed his contract.

"I'd planned to reveal news of your son's death when you won your last match and blame it on Mizra. The vengeance fight between the two of you would have been the biggest draw. Grief would have fueled you and then I would have detonated the explosive in your wrist for a final farewell in the arena. But the stupid Nagani killed Mizra."

Hearing Garod coldly recite his plan stunned Farid. There was no remorse or guilt in his voice. He'd intended to lie about

Turin's death to instigate fake drama for entertainment. No concern for the pain Farid would have suffered.

"You were going to kill me?" Farid asked as the realization sunk in.

The grin stretching Garod's face spoke of more than greed. It was heartless. "Then I would have had your son to raise into the next great champion."

Which was why Farid had begged Sora to take him. He'd known as soon as he saw the caretaker bring his son out that whatever Garod had planned wouldn't be in Turin's best interest. Farid didn't care about what happened to him. He cared about Turin. Only his son mattered.

"The boy is gone?" Parson screeched, looking wildly around. "He was ours!"

"The conglomerate doesn't own my son. They never did," Farid snapped.

Garod continued to grin. His eyes gleamed down at Farid who still held him aloft effortlessly. "If I can't have him, no one can."

Then to Farid's horror, Garod flicked his thumb over the glowing red icon. Farid dropped Garod and reached anxiously for the comm device but it was too late. The message on the screen held a single phrase. *Detonation complete.*

The caretaker let out a pained cry. Farid roared. "What did you do?"

Laughter spilled from Garod as he tipped his head back from his sprawled position on the floor. "Now...now, h-h-he really is dead. You killed your own son by sending him away."

More laughter and Farid's only thought was of stopping the maniacal sound. He raised his leg to stomp Garod in the face.

Weapons powered on and the new guards entering aimed for Farid.

"Don't kill him! We need him!" Bindor yelled.

Pain ripped down Farid's spine. Electrical currents zinged up and down his back. Farid's last thought before he dropped to the floor was of his son. What was the range on the device and had Sora gotten him far enough away?

Chapter 21

1 week later

"So they basically poisoned him," Sora muttered upon hearing the news from Tagan.

Sitting at the table in her room, Turin devoured a bowl of leafy greens and tore through a platter of fruits and vegetables.

Kelix came over to stand next to Sora and Tagan. His tone stayed even so as not to alert Turin who kept turning a wary eye in their direction. "Gurzals follow a strict plant based diet by nature not choice.

"Their bodies can't process large quantities of meat. According to the medical scans, the level of meat found in Turin's stomach was above and beyond what he should even have attempted to consume in a year."

"They had to know he was sickening. His size alone would have told them," Sora whispered harshly. Thinking of what could have happened to an innocent child set flames to her ire all over again.

In the week he'd been with them, Turin's form had already filled out, his green and brown skin taking on a rich camouflage tone more in line with his race. There was a vibrancy to his eyes that hadn't been there before. Like now. He bounced in his seat, feet tapping on the floor as he forked a large leaf covered in a flavored sauce into his mouth.

"There was top of line medical on that ship. Every fighter got routine scans and injuries were seen to immediately," Kelix said.

Tagan frowned. "Could they have missed it?"

He'd become taken with the boy, working hard to gain his trust by visiting Sora's rooms and simply talking to him.

In the beginning, Turin wouldn't let Sora out of his sight. She wasn't sure what had created the strong attachment he held toward her but the feeling was reciprocated and her cyborg heart already overflowed with love for him.

Kelix snorted. "If they knew anything about Gurzals, they would have noticed."

Surely Farid would have told them. He would have had the same dietary requirements. She remembered the trip to the kitchen and the cook who prepared food he could eat when it was late. Thinking of him caused a twinge in the upper region of her chest. She massaged the area. "Any word on where the *Gladyx* is?"

Cyllus rubbed his hands together, his brown gold eyes glinting. "The tracker I managed to plant on the hull of the ship is still emitting a signal plus the one you installed in their drive. We know exactly where they are and they didn't reach Hanass yet."

Relief filled Sora at the news. Since leaving Farid and the *Gladyx* she'd been consumed with the need to go back. Wondering what happened after they left was driving her insane. She didn't know if he was alive or dead.

"How's the handsome boy today?" Savannah "Savie" Monroe called out as she strolled in with her ever present smile.

Turin finished eating and stood. He didn't move from the table but it was clear he itched to go to the Earth woman. "Hi, Savie."

Savie made a beeline for the boy and hugged him tight before ruffling his hair. "Are you ready to go for that visit today?"

She was taking him to see Thalen. Turin appeared fascinated with Sora's pod member and insisted Thalen was going to wake soon.

"That's my cue," Cyllus chimed in with a ready grin.

Cyllus didn't need to accompany them but wanted to be present in case Turin *was* right and the other cyborg woke up confused and attacked the strangers near him.

He curved an arm around Savie's shoulder and propped his other hand on the top of Turin's head. "We won't be gone long."

Long enough for Sora, Kelix and Tagan to devise a plan to go back and rescue Farid. They didn't want Turin to know in case things didn't work out.

Or Farid was dead.

The door closed behind the trio and Sora exhaled. She moved toward the table and cleaned up the mess and dishes. "We need to consider Reo too."

Tagan growled under his breath. "I can't believe he was on the *Gladyx* and never connected with you and Kelix to say something."

"I had meetings with him twice and never once suspected the buyer Kona was Reo. His skin masking was excellent work," Kelix grumbled.

Once she'd put things to right, Sora arched an eyebrow and leaned back against the table, hands gripping the edge. "He had to have another on him as well as an alternate identity prepared. The transporter belt is only good for short range."

Reo had followed through on his promise and sent a contact comm code to Tagan through an untraceable source. They didn't want to use it yet in case it jeopardized his position.

"At least we know he's alive," Kelix continued with a sigh.

It had bothered him not knowing where the other cyborg was. Kelix had leader written all over him though Cyllus had been the original head of their pod grouping. There was an ease to him now that Xion and Kaito were back. The completion of a pod could do that to you. It was like being surrounded by family.

"He owes us for leaving without a word and I'm not going to let him forget," Tagan grumbled.

Sora snorted. "None of us will. When do we leave and how are we doing this?"

They huddled together and outlined the parameters of a straight forward seek and blow mission. Seek the enemy. Blow things up. Sora knew it well.

In the end it was decided that Sora and Kelix would go.

"I should go too," Tagan protested. "I'm an explosives expert."

Sora shook her head. "Kelix is right. He and I already know the layout of the *Gladyx*. We can get in and out with Farid in less time than it would take for you to figure things out."

Tagan glared. "Because the non-organic computer part of my brain wouldn't be able to memorize that?"

Kelix laughed outright. "You know the reason. It's why we didn't select you before. Your emotions operate at an intense level. We can't risk it."

For some reason, the conversion had minimized their stronger emotions but Tagan's had come through more volatile.

As if becoming a cyborg *enhanced* his already hot tempered nature.

"Besides, we need you to get Kaito and Xion acclimated to Solus."

Tagan shot Kelix a dark look for that comment. Finally he blew out a breath. "Fine. I'll stay here. I can keep Turin company. Teach him a few fight moves."

"No!" Sora blurted then flushed to the roots of her hair when they stared at her in surprise. "I'm not sure his father wants him taking part in anything close to fighting."

If Farid didn't come through this, Sora had every intention in keeping Turin and she'd raise him the way his father would have wanted. Farid spent ten years working toward his freedom and his son's. As far as she was concerned that included making sure the child had a semblance of peace in his life.

"Defending himself is a good skill to have. There are many more like those who run the *Gladyx*. I won't teach him anything yet but think about what happened to us. Without our skills, Shui would have decimated a large contingent of our Military Elite and most of that cyborg soldiers."

Tagan's words resonated and Sora understood his point. She needed to think on it more. Hopefully, they'd be returning with his father and Farid could decide on his own.

Kelix cleared his throat, drawing her attention. "We'll let the others know."

Clenching her fingers at her side, then forcing them loose, Sora straightened from her slouch against the table. "Alright. We leave tomorrow. Take the ship. Go in under the radar and recover Farid. Then out fast and hard even if it means lasers blazing."

Tagan and Kelix nodded, speaking at the same time. "Exactly.

***

Slinking along the wall on the lower level of the *Gladyx*, Sora tapped her ear comm and received a single tap in return. Against their better judgment, she and Kelix had to split up to find Farid. His rooms were empty and diving into security onboard the ship hadn't helped to locate him.

Sora headed for the cages and cells under the arena while Kelix made his way to the suite of rooms used by the conglomerate members.

Unlike before, there were three guards stationed in front of the gated doorway to the tunneled section. She placed her palm on the wall near an open outlet and pushed a measured amount of energy through.

The lights above flickered and the lock on the gate clicked. The taller guard glanced at his two peers. "What was that?"

One of them responded, "Not sure, Jimson. Should we notify Garod?"

Jimson nodded. "Garod said he wanted to be told about any and all disturbances."

The trio drifted away and as soon as her auditory senses could no longer hear the tread of their steps, Sora advanced and opened the gate. She slid through while it was still in motion.

"I'm in the cells beneath the arena. Three guards on alert," she reported to Kelix in a low murmur.

His whispered response was just as quiet. "Nothing on my end."

Farid had to be down here. Sora refused to consider the possibility that he might be dead. She hurried down the center aisle skimming close along one side, ignoring the grunts and snores of the fighters sleeping. None of them housed Farid.

She neared the cages toward the end and slowed. The Doorian stood in one smooth motion and dipped his head to the left. "You're back. He is there, though I'm not sure he'll survive the night."

Sora followed the direction he signaled and a tiny cry escaped. She flew the last steps to the cage on the very end. Sprawled on the floor with matted hair covering his face was Farid. Blood pooled around him and bruises bloomed across his bare chest. His pants were torn and stained, the animal skull on his belt chipped.

Another pulse of energy and the bars rattled open. Farid didn't move. Sora ran to his side and kneeled next to his prone form. A quick internal scan revealed three cracked ribs, dislocated left shoulder, two broken fingers that appeared to have been stomped and a broken nose.

Her sensors pulled a deeper report and the data scrolled across her ocular implant. He needed help right away. She tapped the comm behind her ear. "Found him but he's been beaten severely and has multiple broken bones."

Kelix's replied in an instant. "On my way."

"Alright," Sora whispered to Farid. "We need to get you out of here."

But how was the question. She slid an arm under his shoulder and lifted him into an upright position. She'd carry him all the way if she had to.

"Let me out and I won't sound an alarm," Bommba said from behind her.

Sora glanced over her shoulder. The Doorian stood at the front of his cage, hands clasped around the bars and anxiously watching her. Ripped muscles lined his lean frame and he'd proven to be an apt fighter according to the three matches he'd had since her escape with the others.

He was still an unknown though. "How do I know I can trust you and you won't yell the moment I open your cage?"

Cocking his head to the side and staring with single minded intensity through his one eye, he shrugged. "You don't."

Fuck. Sora lowered Farid carefully back to the ground and went across to Bommba's cage. She glared. "I will hunt you to the end of the galaxy if you betray me."

A touch of her hand to the lock and the bars of his cage swung wide. He blinked then took a deep breath. "Let's hurry. Garod has been expecting you to return for Farid."

Sora went back to lift Farid. He groaned and his head sagged forward on his chest. Concern shot through her. "What did they do to him?"

"Which time?" Bommba asked with a snort. "When he refused to fight? When he stood in the arena and laughed as opponent after opponent was brought out?"

Anger bubbled up through her skin. Sora pushed it down with a thought and hefted Farid out of the blood stained cage and over her left shoulder.

When they reached the aisle, Kelix appeared in front of them, a laser gripped in each hand and a smear of blood on his cheek. "Is he good to go?"

"He's hurt bad," Sora said.

"I've got a nanobot injector if you want to try that," Kelix offered, tucking one of the lasers away and pulling out the vile to toss her way.

Sora caught it in her free hand. Before she could try and wake Farid, alarms blared all over.

"A minute. We need to move faster than this," she muttered, coming to a stop. As much as she didn't want to hurt him more than he already was, his life was at stake. Bommba's single brow arched in question but she didn't have time to explain. She adjusted her hold to shift Farid over her shoulders in a carry that placed his weight across her back and left his legs and arms dangling. One hand clamped down on his upper thighs and the other gripped his arm. "Let's go!"

With Kelix maintaining the lead, they took off running. Not toward the docking bay. Garod would be expecting them to go that way if he suspected they came to rescue Farid. It's why they'd come through an unused bio-waste shaft. Her thighs burned as she ran and Farid's weight added to her load.

Ignoring the screeching alarms assaulting her ears, Sora slowed behind Kelix when he reached their earlier entry point. Every breath a pant, she waited while he eased the door open. Bommba paused and grimaced. "This is a waste tunnel."

Sora rolled her eyes. "It's not like we're going to open any of the ship evac tubes to clean them."

Bommba continued to hesitate. "The other side ends in open space unless we're going to crawl around inside and hide."

His disgusted expression conveyed his thoughts on that. Kelix huffed a breath and shoved him aside to crawl through.

Sora tipped sideways to get Farid's legs in without bumping the walls and proceeded to follow.

Bommba grabbed her arm and she snapped. "Listen. We don't have time to appease your delicate sensibilities. Our ship is locked to the hull with a mag-grapple connector. You can come with us or take your chances and remain here. Whatever you decide, get your fucking hand off of me."

To add emphasis to the demand, she let energy flare beneath her skin and he yanked his hand away on a yelp, shaking the burning fingers. Sora went inside the tunnel and worried about Farid's unconscious state. Other than a groan from being jostled, he didn't make any sounds or try to speak.

Chapter 22

Inside the tunnel, cool air wafted through but beneath the manufactured currents, Sora caught the acrid odor from the evac tubes.

This area ran the length of the ship and recycled waste was processed through a network of tubing. Once a week the environmental staff came through and cleaned out whatever didn't break down fully. It was a dirty job but had to be done. Blocked evac or waste tubing could turn into a full blown nightmare on an epic scale for a ship this size.

Halogen lights gave off a golden glow, illuminating Kelix's rushing form. He'd kicked on the cyborg speed and Sora matched him step for step. Bommba trailed behind but she didn't have time to worry about him.

They finally reached the end of the twisting tunnel and the suits they'd used to cross between the small gap caused by the mag-grapple hook to their ship outside. Sora lowered Farid carefully and picked up the silver material. She dressed as fast as possible and zipped up the front.

She kneeled next to Farid to put him in the spare suit they'd brought with them. His eyes popped open. Fear and desperation glowed from within. "Turin. Did my son make it?"

The explosive implanted in his wrist. Farid had no idea if Garod had detonated the device and if his son survived. If Sora had to guess, she bet the conglomerate leader had taunted Farid with that very thing.

"Safe. No explosive device or tracking mechanism," she rushed to assure him. Then smiled. "Looking for his father who made him a promise."

"Sora! Hurry!" Kelix called.

Kelix had his safety suit on and sealed, the matching helmet under his arm. Sora faced Farid again. He braced a hand on the ground and pushed up. She caught his shoulder. "Be careful."

"No time," he muttered and staggered to his feet on a shaky exhale. "You came back."

It was a statement made in wonder. A tremulous smile crossed Sora's lips. She'd been afraid of facing his condemnation. "I came back."

Bommba watched and the calculating gleam in his eye put Sora on alert. His gaze shifted in her direction and she said "Try it."

He flushed and smoothed a hand over his head.

"We can't leave yet," Farid said when she held up the spare suit for him.

"What do you mean?!"

His expression hardened. "I'm not leaving until Garod is dead."

"Is he serious?" Kelix asked

Farid drew a deep breath then shuddered from the effort and leaned on a lower tube. "The other members can wait but Garod leads them, Garod controls the credits. Without him, they're easier to pick off."

"You're in no condition to face him, Farid!"

His busted lips curved upward. "That's why I have you. I'm not the only one with a promise to keep."

Sora's belly quivered. Damn him.

"Sora, decision time. We have to roll." Kelix's voice vibrated with urgency.

"This is my cue to exit," Bommba interrupted. He tipped his head toward Sora. "My thanks."

Then took off back the way they came. Sora focused on her friend. "Go, Kelix. We all can't be caught."

He stared hard, his reluctance clear. "You sure abut this?"

"We'll make our way there. This needs to be done first," Sora informed him.

Kelix cursed then jammed the helmet on his head. "Don't make us have to come after you. Farid, if anything happens to her..."

"If anything happens to either of us, take care of my son for me." Farid's words caused Kelix to stiffen.

Another growled curse and then he went through the hatch, slamming the door behind him. The vacuum seal activated and Sora watched through the glass window as he bounced and hopped his way to the shuttle on the other side.

***

Farid clasped a hand to his waist. Something was definitely broken. The only reason he managed to stay on his feet was due to his years of fighting through extreme pain. So while he was in agony, he could move. *Would* move.

"This is a bad idea," Sora said after the rumble of her friend's ship outside faded.

Ignoring the glare she aimed his way, Farid moved closer to her. Sending Turin with Sora had been a spur of the moment decision. He'd only had seconds to react. Trust didn't come easy but Farid saw the guilt and worry in Sora's gaze at Garod's revelation.

It was enough to convince him that no one else was more worthy to get his son away. She hadn't failed him. His only concern had been if they were still in range when Garod triggered the explosive. "Is my son really okay?"

The frustration on her face eased. She tentatively touched his bare arm and leaned forward to stare directly into his eyes. "I wouldn't lie about that. No matter what happened before. Turin is fine.

"You have my word as a member of the Cyborg Military Elite. There are two overprotective cyborgs with him at all times. I wouldn't have left him if I didn't believe one hundred percent that your son was in good hands."

And that was why he'd told her to take Turin. The glimpses of that dedicated honor.

"Listen, about what Garod said," she started.

Farid shook his head. "We can talk about that later but I don't take anything the conglomerate tells me at face value. If you lied about Turin's death for a reason, it had to be a good one."

Her lips parted then she clutched at him. "That's just it. It wasn't a lie. I was specifically told—"

The screeching alarms suddenly went silent. Sora's gaze automatically jerked up toward the elaborate network of pipes above them. The quiet was unnerving.

"What happened?" he asked.

Sora's hand moved from his arm to his mouth, covering Farid's lips. Her features strained as she focused. Had Garod discovered their presence?

"If we're to do what we intend, we need to do it now," she whispered. "Garod will realize you're not in the cage and sensors will indicate a ship took off from this side of the *Gladyx*."

"Then we need to be quick."

"Wait." Sora unclasped a small tube from the belt at her waist. She held it between two fingers and extended it to him. "Kelix gave me this for you. It's a nanobot injector. I didn't want to use it while you were unconscious in case Gurzals are sensitive to foreign bodies introduced into their systems."

Farid glanced at the tiny tube and the speckles of gold slivers floating inside a clear liquid. He knew about nanobots. They aided in repairing internal damage. The medical center had never offered them to him for fear it would impact his ability to fight if his system fought the aggressive healing nature of them.

Taking the tube from her, Farid rolled it in the palm of his hand.

"Is it safe, Farid?"

His lips curled up at the corner as he met her gaze. "We're about to find out."

Before Sora could think to stop him, Farid jammed the injector into his left forearm. The tube emptied quickly.

"Farid!" Her eyes widened and she growled under her breath. "I guess that's one way to find out."

He chuckled, allowing the burn of the nanobots to work their way through his body. "If it helps me to get out of here, it was worth it."

Something he couldn't identify flickered in her gaze, a softening only to be replaced with the hard glint of duty. She shoved at his side and squeezed around him to head back the way they'd come through the tunnels. "Move. Taking the cameras down doesn't mean they can't figure out where we are."

Pushing past his pain, Farid followed. They reached the entrance and Sora kicked the door open with no mind to stealth. She bared her teeth in a wicked grin. "We can't hide with the alarms going off so let's give Garod something to worry about. Today is his last day to live."

Fire bubbled beneath Farid's skin. His broken ribs fused together with painful, grinding jolts. The bruises on his face swelled and faded as the vessels beneath his skin knit back together.

Each wound and break healed by the nanobots sent pain ripping across his body and left his head throbbing from the speed of the forced unnatural act. He gritted his teeth against the agony and kept up with Sora as she charged into the open hall.

A laser was pressed into his hand and she aimed the one she held at the rapidly approaching guards in uniform. Without hesitation, she fired.

The guards dropped to the floor before they could aim in their direction. Admiration flared but Farid had no time to speak of it. More guards poured into the area and Sora became a machine in truth. With a laser in one hand she fired blast after blast, tearing through the ranks.

She used the blade in her other hand to swipe the throat of one guard on the right and slash the thigh of another on the left.

Farid aided her as best he could shooting any new arrivals but the swiftness with which Sora took down the dozen guards attested to her cyborg abilities. Farid was no match for that level of speed. Smoke billowed around them from the chaos she created and he found himself reluctantly grinning as he joined in the fray, taking out the two guards she'd missed.

At the door that led into the restricted hall, he paused beside Sora and eyed her from head to toe. No gasping or panting. Her gaze remained solid and clear. She wore her black hair up in a pony tail but long strands fell about her face obscuring the CR brand.

No facial prosthetic coverings. No hiding who or what she was.

"Are you alright?" she asked, eyeing him with the same intense study he'd given her.

He nodded. "Let's go."

Chapter 23

Adrenalin ebbed and flowed within Sora but she suppressed it easily and focused on the promise she'd made Farid. Two promises actually. One to Turin to bring his father back and the one she'd made to Farid vowing to kill Garod.

She planned to uphold both of those commitments today. Racing down the hall with Farid at her side, Sora led them to the off-limits section of the ship for VIP, buyers and the conglomerate members.

Getting through the locks was nothing. When she reached the final turn, she drew up short. Garod stood in front of the door to his room, hands shoved into the pockets of his black pants and a wide grin on his face. "I've been waiting for you to come back."

She braced her weight evenly on her legs and matched her smile to his. "Glad to be back."

He snort laughed then his gaze shifted to Farid and narrowed. "I'm surprised you're up. Pleased but surprised."

At her side, Farid's upper lip curled. "I've taken worse beatings in the ring than what you gave."

Sora stiffened. Garod had been the one to beat Farid. Her grip tightened on the laser she held but she didn't fire. Garod shrugged. "A slight miscalculation on my part. I didn't want to ruin my investment. It would have been glorious for the fans to see you go down in the arena during a death match."

The clock was ticking. Sora had no doubt Garod was planning something and this was his way of stalling them. She had promises to keep. Waving her laser at him, Sora said, "This can be simple or difficult."

Garod smirked. "Oh, I'm sure it's going to be very difficult. For Farid that is. He seems to have developed feelings for you. We'll see how long they last when it's you against him in the arena. Imagine it—the cyborg on the run, facing our undefeated champion."

Never. Sora would never fight Farid or participate in these illegal games. "Authorities have been alerted to the location of the *Gladyx*. To make matters worse, your crimes involved a child. For that, I sentence you to death."

The whine of lasers powering on behind her filled the air. Sora didn't turn. She knew who the real threat was.

Garod waved a hand, holding the guards off and shook his head. "Poor Turin. I had such great plans for him. Too bad he didn't live to see the day."

A cold ugly knot twisted in Sora's belly. Her immediate reaction was to deny the claim. If they hadn't scanned Farid's son, if she hadn't been able to destroy the explosive, Garod would have killed him. She thought of the future and how this assumption could give Farid and Turin a bit of freedom.

Instead of bragging about Turin's survival she let the hatred she felt inside rise. Her gaze never left Garod's cruel stare as he taunted Farid. Before she killed him, she intended to get answers. "Why did you have worker in the care center tell me of Turin's death? Why lie?"

Garod rubbed his palms together, glanced subtly at the comm on his wrist then answered her. "Actually she really thought the child was dead. A I told, Farid, I planned to blame

Mizra and use Farid's rage as motivation to set up an epic fight between them but you ruined that."

"You were willing to play with my son's life," Farid snarled from beside her.

"It's not personal. Just business." Again, Garod shrugged. "After you died in the ring, I would have waited a few years then announced Turin as an upcoming fighter on a path to avenge his father and claim his title as champion."

Turin was *ten.* A child! Her hand trembled on her weapon. Would he have forced the boy to fight while he was still young? The evil look in his eyes assured Sora of exactly that. Thinking of the child who'd clutched her in terror, the fear when he'd asked if his father was alive—all of it solidified what Sora needed to do.

"Sora, you need to get your ass out of there. An elite division of Kirsian guards are on target to reach the *Gladyx* in exactly twelve minutes," Kelix suddenly blasted in her ear comm.

Elation soared. Apparently, the protective fool hadn't left her. She fired directly at Garod. Her aim was perfect and the blast sheared the right side of his throat and the quivering spikes. Blood sprayed in an arc. He was dead before he hit the floor.

She grabbed Farid's arm and took him down to the floor as the guards opened fire. Leaning on her hip with one arm braced over Farid's torso, Sora sighted and took each of them down. She pulled Farid back to his feet. "Get up! Get up!"

He looked at the dead men. "That wasn't how I expected things to go."

"The emperor from my planet has sent a ship with a unit on its way. We need to get off the *Gladyx*."

"What about the other members of the conglomerate?" he asked, following her as she headed to the docking bay.

Unlike last time, she took the lift. They dropped quickly and the doors opened on the correct floor.

"They aren't here. I scanned the doors as we passed the rooms and they were all empty. I think Garod sent them away temporarily. He knew I'd come back for you and planned this well."

Sora spied a two-seater shuttle and went straight toward it. It wasn't for long range travel but she just needed it to get her to Kelix and their ship. Farid eyed the smaller vessel. "Are you certain this is a good idea?"

She grinned as they climbed in and strapped up. The clear roof lowered, sealing them in. "We don't need to go far. Kelix is here."

The corner of Farid's lips ticked up. "You have good friends. What about everyone else here on the *Gladyx*?"

"Oh, don't worry. The ship isn't going anywhere. The authorities know exactly where to find them thanks to a tracker we planted when we were here last. The *Gladyx* will limp into a port for repairs due to the electrical issues I created before. That's where those guilty will be apprehended and everyone else will be free to go or sign on with a *legal* fight venue."

***

Farid couldn't believe this was happening. Sora piloted the shuttle with a skill he admired then aligned the emergency hatch next to a sleek armored black ship outside the *Gladyx*. The seal snapped in place and a doorway opened on the other side, allowing them to abandon the two-seater and board the larger vessel.

A thud sounded from behind him as the doorway close. Through the glass, Farid watched the two-seater grow smaller and smaller as they moved away. Turning back around, he breathed deeply of the recycled air minus the heavy cleaning products he'd become accustomed to scenting. This was his first time off of the *Gladyx* since he'd signed his contract to free Ashme.

"Are you okay?" Sora asked beside him.

A smile stretched his lips and Farid grabbed her around the waist and pulled her in close. He pressed his mouth to hers and kissed her hard and quick. She didn't push away but a sizzling zap in his midsection reminded him of the nanobots working feverishly to repair his body.

The lights above glowed brightly then dimmed. His vision hazed and nausea swirled in his belly. Familiar with the sensation after many fights, Farid managed to mutter, "Yes, but I'm going to pass out."

"Farid!"

Sora called his name and the world went dark.

Chapter 24

Farid awoke in an instant. He glanced around from the narrow bed and spied the medical equipment around him. The door swished open and Sora's friend entered.

"You're up."

"Yeah." Farid cleared the rasp from his throat and pushed himself upright. "Are we clear?"

The dark-haired cyborg came toward Farid with a handheld scanner. "We're far enough away you don't have to worry about the conglomerate coming for you."

That didn't mean much. Wait. The explosive. Farid clasped his wrist. "There's an explosive implanted to keep fighters from escaping the *Gladyx*."

He received a grim smile. "Sora took care of that when you did your face dive."

Heat filled his cheeks. "Where are we headed?"

"We are on our way to the temporary base we set up."

Sora's explanation had Farid's head jerking toward the door. She strolled in with the sexy walk he remembered from the first time they'd met. "And Turin?"

His son was foremost in his mind. Sora stopped at his side and stroked a hand through his hair. Farid leaned into the touch. "Safe. We'll be with him in a few short minutes."

Minutes. His heart skipped then thudded hard in his chest. How long had he been out?

"Hours," her friend said.

Farid must have spoken aloud.

"Farid, this is Kelix or as you knew him Durwin," Sora said, settling on the bed beside him.

"Thank you," Farid told the other man gratefully.

Kelix grinned and shrugged. "Sora was determined. We all vowed to stick together so no way I was leaving her behind."

"I'm glad you didn't," Sora added.

"I'll leave you two alone. We should reach Solus soon."

As soon as Kelix left, Farid reached for Sora's hand and held tight. "I don't know how to thank you for everything you did."

She leaned forward and kissed him on the side of his head. "No thanks are needed. You helped me and I helped you."

It was more than that. She'd saved his life, saved his son's life.

"Get some rest," she said. "You have a very excited boy waiting to see you."

Farid grinned. He was finally free.

***

Solus was slowly feeling like home. Sora understood it was a temporary base until they could return to Kirs but there was something about the colony that grew on her. Or maybe it was the bond growing between her and the other cyborgs she'd come to depend on.

Turin burst into the front door of the suite of rooms they lived in, a wide grin splitting his face. "Thalen couldn't find me for thirty minutes."

Seated on the sofa, Farid chuckled as his son ran over to him and wrapped his arms about his hips. He leaned over and hugged him back. "You're getting better."

Thalen had awakened strangely enough just as Turin had said. Turin's fascination with the severely injured cyborg didn't have an explanation. Thalen for his part seemed to be equally fascinated with the child and succumbed to the constant pleading to play hiding games while Turin tried to hone his camouflage skills.

Farid had played once with all the other cyborgs and despite their sensors, none had been able to discover his presence for hours. When he'd returned, everyone expressed their admiration and now Turin wanted to excel in the same manner.

"I want to be great!" Turin declared then dashed back out the open door.

Turin had adapted quickly. The child loved having a circle of "powerful" friends, as he called them, watching over him. He thrived being surrounded by the cyborgs and knowing he had the freedom and access to go into any of the suites on their floor of the housing building.

Sora shook her head and scooted over on the cushions until her side aligned with Farid's. He wrapped his arm about her shoulders and kissed the top of her head. She'd never get used to the affection. Or maybe she would. There had been many late night talks. Sharing of their personal worries.

Sora listened to the painful story of how Farid ended up fighting on the *Gladyx* and he listened as she talked about the emperor's plot and the tragedy she'd taken part of on Bionus. Together they grieved their actions that caused death for many and together they worked to heal the wounds they each still suffered.

The block on her emotions had also been cracked wide open. Her feelings poured through in large waves at intervals. One moment Sora found herself laughing constantly at Turin's antics but just as easily she could end up prostrate on the bed crying for her missing pod brethren.

Through it all, Farid stood by her. He soothed, encouraged and mostly stayed quiet while holding her during the worst of it.

For her part, when he woke from nightmares and thought he was still on the *Gladyx*, she distracted him with sex. It might seem odd to some but the physical exertions brought him back from the past better than anything else they'd tried. On those nights, they'd both end up entwined in one another's arms, shaking and exhausted.

"Found him!" Tagan exclaimed, poking his head in the doorway.

Sora rolled her eyes. "Who did you find?"

"Reo," Kelix answered, shoving Tagan to the side to come in.

Cyllus and Savie followed with Savie wiggling her fingers in greeting.

Tension lined Farid's body. Sora reached over and squeezed his leg. He wasn't always comfortable with the ease with which they entered one another's space. Sora understood his time on the *Gladyx* had more to do with those feelings than any true concern about the others.

"Where is Reo?" she asked, sitting forward in eagerness.

"Quator," Tagan said with relish.

Sora frowned. She wasn't familiar with the location.

"He sent a coded message but I broke it down and backtracked the source. He tried to hide it but made a simple error." Tagan's joy couldn't be contained as he reported the information.

Cyllus sat and pulled Savie onto his lap. "How soon can we go and retrieve him?"

Sora laughed but Farid asked in a serious tone. "What if he doesn't want to come back?"

They all stared at him. Farid shrugged. "He left for a reason. If finding these women will bring him peace, why not help him instead of forcibly making him return to Solus?"

Kelix blinked. "Fuck."

"I agree with, Farid," Savie said.

Savie and Reo had developed an odd bond when she'd been rescued from a failed science experiment. No one truly understood how or what had created the connection but Savie's presence had definitely brought parts of Reo back.

Sighing, Cyllus rubbed Savie's back. "Looks like we have a new plan."

A relieved breath slid from Farid. Sora glanced at him but as usual he masked his expression in front of her friends. They'd talk later and she'd get him to discuss further any concerns he had. For now, she was pleased he'd spoken up.

"Are going to talk about Xion and Kaito?" Cyllus asked next.

The two men had obviously been changed by their experience. According to Kelix and Cyllus, Xion was quieter than he'd been before the treason charge but it was Kaito they worried about the most.

He didn't speak or leave his room other than to respond to Kelix's demands for a welfare check on his status. Kaito also refused to open his NNP up fully to his pod which was an extreme concern.

Sora didn't know what he'd been like before but she'd witnessed the first and only match he'd been in on the *Gladyx*. Zozo's death had done something to Kaito and being forced to kill Bindor had exacerbated it. She only hoped he'd be able to resolve his feelings and remain stable.

"I think we need to give those two more time. Let's focus on helping Reo."

Since Sora agreed with Kelix, she nodded, "I second this."

The others chimed in and soon departed. When they were alone, Sora swiveled about on the sofa. "Okay?"

Farid's smile was small but there. "Very okay."

Taking a deep breath, she asked, "Do we need to talk about last night?"

Specifically, Farid telling Sora he wanted to explore a deeper relationship and where it might lead with her.

He ran a hand up and down her arm, leaving goosebumps in his wake. "I think the bigger question is do *you* need to talk about last night. We already know where I stand."

She swallowed. Her last official romantic relationship had been years ago. To accept what Farid offered scared her and she wasn't ashamed to say it. "I'm...terrified."

His smile widened, gained in its sincerity. "Me too. Does it help knowing that?"

She laughed. "No."

Farid pulled her over to straddle his lap, her legs bracketing his thighs. She set her hands on his broad shoulders and exhaled. "I don't mean to be difficult. Everything has happened so fast. Not just between us but with my pod. Thalen's awakening..."

A firm finger tapped her lips, stopping the stream of words spilling from her mouth. "Do you want Turin and I to find our own space?"

The thought sent her heart racing. "No. Stay. I want both of you living with me."

The way they already were. Turin didn't seem to care. He had his papa back and got to keep an eye on Sora.

Farid's thumb caressed her chin then stroked over to the CR mark on her face. "Do you care about me, Sora?"

A knot lodged in her throat but she pushed past it. "So much. I care about you so much."

He dropped his hand from her face and kissed her lightly. "Then that's all we deal with right now because you know I care about you too. One step, one day, at a time."

Her shoulders slumped and she leaned forward to nestle her face in the crevice created between his shoulder and the base of his throat. "Thank you for understanding me."

He caressed her back, the weight of his warm palms, lulling her into a sense of calm. "Always."

Sora had no doubt this was exactly where she was meant to be. With Farid.

Author's Note

Hello, readers. Cyborgs! This time, a female one. LOL. I like strong women as much as I like women being rescued by the hero. Sora allowed me to do a bit of both. She and Farid were an intriguing couple to put together and helping them fall in love left me feeling happy. I also adored the little glimpses of Turin.

As to what's next on the horizon, I love the plans I'm in the process of making and can't wait to share. 2022 is looking like a full load with lots of passionate romances coming your way.

For more information about upcoming books, who's next or excerpts, sign up for my newsletter via my site. I'm moving a lot of those details to my website with the exclusive content like cover reveals and sneak peeks going to my subscribers.

Other books in the Cyborg Redemption series if you haven't tried them are available. *His Cold Kiss* by Michelle Howard, *Saving Her Cyborg* by AM Griffin, *Hijacked* by Lolita Lopez, *True as Steel* by Regine Abel.

Oh and follow me on IG if you want to see random pics of my life. LOL. As always, reviews on retailer sites about your enjoyment of the books are always welcome.

Thanks for reading,

Michelle

About the Author

USA Best Selling Author, Michelle Howard lives in a happy fantasy world where she writes sci-fi and paranormal based romances. Love stories have been a staple in her life since she discovered some of her favorite romance novels by classic authors like Judith McNaught, Julie Garwood and Johanna Lindsey.

I love to hear from fans so please reach out to me. If the mood hits you, leave a review.

Email: michellehowardwrites@gmail.com
Instagram: @mhowardwrites
Website: www.michellehowardwrites.com
Sign up for my newsletter via my website

Also by Michelle Howard

A Novel of the Dracol

Rylin's Fire

Relentless Fire

Frost Fire

Secret Fire

Assassins Guild

The Unexpected Bonding Vow

Claiming His Unexpected Baby

His Unexpected Mate

A World Beyond

Torkel's Chosen

Torkels Auserwählte

Arak's Love

Arak's Liebe

Lindsey's Rescue

Kyele's Passion

Rydak's Fall
Jaron's Promise
V'hor's Nestmate
Stolen Moments
Bane's Heart
Nikol's Surrender

Cyborg Redemption
His Cold Kiss
Her Cold Heart

Le Cœur dans les étoiles
Union à tout prix
Amour à toute épreuve

Liebe in den Sternen
Animalische Begierde
Einzigartige Liebe

Love in the Stars
Mating Urge
Love Like No Other

Magical Lovers
Djinn Lover
Wicked Lover
Wild Lover

The Vassi Contact
As Darkness Spreads
As Dawn Rises

Un roman de L'univers Dracol
La Flamme de Rylin
La Flamme verte
La Flamme de glace

Un Roman di Dracol
il fuoco di Rylin
Fuoco Implacabile
Fuoco di Ghiaccio

Warlord Series
Honor Bound
The Overlord's Heir

A King's Revenge
Rise of the Shadow Warriors
A Warlord's Heart
Unexpected Bride
Unleashing A Warrior

Wired

Wired for Love

Standalone

No Reason To Run
Project Genesis

Watch for more at www.michellehowardwrites.com.

www.ingramcontent.com/pod-product-compliance
Ingram Content Group UK Ltd.
Pitfield, Milton Keynes, MK11 3LW, UK
UKHW040005200726
13854UKWH00001B/54

9 798201 389758